LEVELED

CATHRYN FOX

COPYRIGHT

Leveled
Copyright 2020 by Cathryn fox
Published by Cathryn Fox

ISBN ebook: 978-1-989374-17-7
ISBN Print: 978-1-989374-18-4

JAMIE

Trouble in a bikini.

Yeah, that's what I see from my rooftop vantage point. Trouble in a goddamn bikini, and I don't plan to get within fifty feet of a pretty little rich girl like her. Been there, done that, and have the scars to prove it.

Literally.

I squeeze my fingers around the hammer in my fist, my thoughts racing back to when I was eighteen, specifically to the day I received the shit-kicking of a lifetime. All thanks to a girl no different than the one below me, spread out on her chair without a care in the world as she tans her hot body under the scorching noonday sun.

What I'd do to come face-to-face with my ex's asshole brothers today. Four against one. Yeah, they waited until I was alone and jumped me. Fucking cowards, really. Too afraid of a fair fight, or of facing off against me and my army of brothers. At least I have the satisfaction of knowing I'd broken a few of their noses and cracked a few of their ribs. I can almost hear the bones crunching now.

"Come on, Jamie, you can't tell me you don't want to tap

that," my cousin Ryan says as the blonde shades the sun from her eyes and glances at us before climbing from her lounge chair. I'm pretty sure she just gave an extra shake to her sweet ass as she made her way inside her beachside cottage. Cottage? Okay, more like mansion. Whatever. Doesn't make a difference to me, and she can shake her ass all she wants. That's wasted on me too.

Mostly.

I ignore my twitching cock and with the back of my hand I wipe the perspiration from my forehead and turn to glare at Ryan. "Tap that? No fucking way." I shake my head. Christ, of all the guys—my four brothers and three cousins included—Ryan knows my motto better than any of them: Avoid rich pampered women at all costs. Fuck, man, he was the one who found me in the alleyway and picked my broken and bloodied body up off the ground, all because I messed around with the wrong girl.

A sound catches in my throat. Wrong girl? More like a bored little rich girl who spent the summer slumming with a boy from the wrong side of the tracks, only to end up accusing me of rape when her father walked in on us. Talk about a shit storm of courts and chaos that followed me around after that.

To think I was so young and naïve—stupid really—the two of us talking about a future together. Christ, I was such a fucking dreamer back then. Even my father would get on my case about it. How many times did I drift off in thought when Dad was teaching me construction techniques? Too many to count, that's for sure. But none of that mattered in the end. After the charges were dropped, I left Blue Bay, my days of dreaming and trusting over, but a dark cloud still hangs over my head here in the town where I grew up.

The long-term summer vacationers, who continue to come back year after year from all over the states, will always treat me like I'm a fucking criminal, and I would have stayed in New Orleans for good if my brother Sean hadn't insisted I return home to help with the business after our dad died. I'm doing my part, but that doesn't mean I have to like it. Truthfully, I don't hate it. I had a hammer in my hand before I could fucking talk. We all did. It's just that I prefer the art of tattooing to construction. At least I have my nights and weekends off, and I was able to buy a small space on the other side of town—where the privileged, self-righteous vacationers never venture. Good. I don't need their business, or their support, when I finally get it up and running.

"She's all yours, bro," I say to my cousin Ryan, who'd also returned home at my big brother Sean's insistence. He was a mechanic down in Georgia, but gave it all up in the name of family. "But take my advice, she's got trouble written all over her, and if I were you, I'd stay as far away from her as possible."

He clucks his tongue and grabs another stack of roofing shingles. He sinks to his knees and pulls a few nails from his tool belt. "Yeah, you're probably right. Who needs that kind of shit in their life, anyway?"

"I sure as hell don't," I say. "Not again." But when I hear a loud shriek coming from the neighboring house—the hot blonde's cottage—every muscle in my body tightens.

"What the fuck?" Ryan asks. He stands and walks over to the edge of the roof with me. Shoulder to shoulder, we go still and listen, but when another loud cry sounds, it prompts me in to action.

"Son of a bitch." I kick my leg out and hurry down the ladder. Ryan's boots echo on the metal rungs as he follows, and he stays tight on my heels as we race to the cottage next door. I peer through her screen door, and even though every instinct I have warns me to run the other way, I was raised better than that, and when push comes to shove, it's not in my nature to turn my back on someone who might need my help. Pampered rich girl or not.

"You okay?" I ask from the other side of the door, and count to three as I wait for an answer. When none comes, I exchange a quick look with Ryan and pull on the handle. With my luck I'll probably get accused of breaking and entering, but I yank it open anyway, worry for the girl's well-being gnawing at my gut. The hinges, rusty from the saltwater spray, groan as I stretch them. "Hello," I call out, and step into the house, which smells like coconut suntan lotion—a scent that takes me back to my days in bed with the girl who fabricated a lie that will forever haunt me.

A loud bang, like something—or someone—is being smashed against the wall, reverberates through me, and without thinking I hurry toward the sound, my work boots scuffing on the polished wood floor. But I'm seriously fucking worried she's being attacked, and I'm not about to stop to take my boots off to save her precious oak from getting damaged. I turn the corner, stop at a bedroom to do a quick scan, but all I see is a sewing machine, a dummy with a dress draping off it, and spools of threads and material everywhere. I continue down the hall and stop at the second bedroom. I grip the doorframe and air leaves my lungs in a whoosh when I see what all the commotion is about.

Fuck. Me. Hard.

I want to turn. I should turn. Actually, I should bolt, leave Blue Bay, Connecticut, for good this time, and never look back. But I don't do any of those things. How the fuck could I possibly think of running when I'm staring at the hottest, most gorgeous naked body I've ever set eyes on? Unable to help myself, I give a fast sweep over her nakedness, taking in her long legs, curvy hips, and small breasts that would fit so nicely in my big hands, or better yet, my mouth.

"Jamie," Ryan says, crashing into me, pushing me a little

farther into the bedroom. I stumble and quickly right myself, but not before I get a whiff of the girl's scent. I breathe in her sweet floral aroma, and it strokes my thickening dick, teases and tortures my last working brain cell. Why again is it I don't do pampered rich girls?

"Oh, shit, sorry," Ryan says, when he glimpses the girl scrambling for her robe, and my thoughts come crashing back to the present.

This time I do look away, and grab Ryan's shoulders to turn him too. "Sorry," I say quickly. "We heard a scream. I thought you were in trouble. Didn't mean to walk in on you like this."

"I . . . it was a spider," she says, her voice as sweet and seductive as the woman herself.

Get your shit together, dude. She's everything you vowed to stay away from.

The whoosh of silk fills the silence as she dresses, and I can't help but envy that robe as it gets to touch her body, shape her curves, slide between her legs.

I'm envying a fucking robe?

"You can turn now," she says quietly.

I slowly inch around, and her blue eyes are wide, alarmed, as her gaze goes from me to Ryan, back to me again. I take a minute to see the situation through her eyes and can understand why she looks so frightened. She's just a tiny thing and both Ryan and I are big men, over six feet and covered in tattoos. We're dressed only in jeans, boots and tool belts, and we're blocking her bedroom doorway. Fuck, if I were her, I'd be scared shitless too. But she has nothing to worry from us. Despite our reputation—poster boys for authority issues—we know right from wrong.

Mostly.

Her gaze leaves mine and travels downward, raking over my bare chest like a hot caress. The fear in her eyes changes to appreciation, and my dick twitches again. Fuck, man, I wish she wasn't looking at me like that. It's making it harder and harder for me, and yeah, when I say harder, I'm talking about my dick. Needing a distraction, I glance away and see shattered glass on her floor.

I clear my throat and hope her gaze stops at my tool belt. No need for her to see my hard-on and get the wrong idea that I might want her. I don't.

"Did you get it?"

"Get what?" she asks, her voice sounding more breathless.

My gaze meets hers again. "The spider."

"Oh." She turns toward the glass. "I hit it with my figurine."

A figurine that probably costs more than I make in a week.

"All right. Everything seems good. Glad you're okay. We'll get out of your way."

I turn, and Ryan is grinning at me. Little fucker knows the girl is getting to me. I give him a shove to set him in to motion, and he walks back into the other room. I'm about to follow when she says, "Can I get you a drink? You look hot . . . I mean, it's hot out and you've been on that roof all morning."

I swallow against a dry throat. "No, I'm good."

"I'm Kylee."

I nod and walk out to the main room, but Ryan is long gone, leaving the two of us alone. Motherfucker. I'm going to kill him.

"And you are . . . ?" she probes.

Leaving.

I scrub my chin again, and as much as I just want to get the hell out of there, I was raised with manners. I know one wouldn't think it to look at me. Christ, I hung out with the toughest bastards in New Orleans, fought alongside the meanest gangs, yet I still don't want to be rude to this girl.

"Jamie."

"Nice to meet you, Jamie. Thanks for coming to my rescue."

"Jamie Owens," I say and wait for a reaction, for it to ring a bell. In two seconds I expect a light bulb to go off and her to shove me out the door.

"Kylee Jensen," she says instead.

Guess she doesn't know the Owens boys' reputation. I suppose that shouldn't surprise me. This cottage just sold, and she's new to the area. She's awfully young to own such a big, expensive place on the ocean, though. Either she has a high-paying job, or Daddy bought it for her. I'm going with the latter. And soon enough she'll learn who I am. When all the regular vacationers return next month or so, she'll be warned away from me and won't dare shake her ass at me or invite me into her house again.

Until then, however . . .

What the fuck?

Until then, I still plan to avoid her.

I just hope Grandma Nellie doesn't take it upon herself to invite the newcomer to any Sunday dinners. She's been known to do that. If she does, I plan to make myself scarce.

Kylee steps up to me and zeroes in on my sugar skull tattoo. She puts her finger on my body and I flinch. Her eyes go wide again and she pulls her hand back fast.

"Sorry." She shakes her head. "I shouldn't have touched you."

"It's fine."

She eyes me for a second, then puts her fingers back on me. Sweet fuck, her fingers are so goddamn warm and soft as she traces the skull tattoo, I can't help but want them on my dick.

"This one is really nice," she says.

"Thanks. I designed it for a client when I owned my shop in New Orleans. Liked it so much, I gave myself one."

Why the fuck am I telling her that?

Her hand drops to her side, and she puts it on her hip. "Wow, a real artist. I'm impressed."

"You should be."

She grins, and despite myself, I grin too. "Modest, I like that," she teases and tightens her robe around her sweet curves. "I almost got a tattoo when I turned eighteen, but my father, the all-powerful Jack Jensen, threatened to disown me."

I nod. "Fathers are protective like that."

She angles her head and her soft curls fall down her slender shoulder. Jesus fuck, what I'd do to twist those long strands around my palm as I fuck her bent over her sofa.

"You sound like you know firsthand."

"I've had a few come into my shop, ready to kill me after inking their daughters. But I don't ink underage girls, and they have to be sober. Still, some fathers want to challenge me."

She frowns, and the deep sadness on her face is like a punch to the gut. What did I say to upset her? And why the fuck does seeing her upset bother me so much?

"That's what my father would have done." She wipes away the sorrow and smiles, but it's forced. Ah, I get it. Daddy issues. All the more reason for me to keep my distance. "He's a bit overprotective." Her big eyes race over my naked chest again.

"There are ways to get around that, you know," I say.

"Yeah?"

My gaze drops, lingers at the juncture between her thighs. "Places to ink where he'll never see."

What the fuck am I doing?

When my gaze returns to hers, there is a pink flush on her

cheeks. It's been a long time since I've seen a girl blush. Damned if it isn't sexy as fuck. She looks over my body again, her eyes questioning.

"What?" I ask.

"I . . . uh . . . was just wondering . . ." She shakes her head. "Nothing. Never mind."

Don't ask, dude. Don't ask. Just leave.

"Wondering what?"

Dammit

"Just . . . where did you put your girl's name?"

I hook my thumbs into my tool belt, needing to restrain my hands before I do something I could only regret later. You know, like pull her to me and see if those lips taste as sweet as they look.

"Nowhere." I don't elaborate, don't tell her ink is permanent and relationships aren't—at least for me they aren't. I'm an Owens. The kind of guy a girl fucks, not one she brings home to Daddy. Especially a protective one like hers.

She toys with the silk belt on her robe. Jesus, one tug and she'd be naked again. "You sure you don't want a drink? It's the least I could do after you ran to my rescue."

The least.

"I'm good." Good? No, not really. I got a fucking monster boner, and that's not good at all. I'm all about fucking, just not girls like her. Jesus, man, I need to get back to work and get back to minding my own business before things take a turn for the worse and I act on my fucking urges. Seems to me like she wants me to, though, from the way she's eye fucking me and all and asking if I have a girl. But I'm done with bored women looking to spice up their dull lives with a little danger. I don't trust her, but more importantly, I don't trust myself around her.

"I better get back to work," I say.

"Before you go, can I . . . ah . . . show you something?"

Yes, please...

I open my mouth, afraid of what's going to come out—yeah, all the blood is in my dick—but I pinch my lips shut when she points toward the ocean. "I was thinking my back deck needs to be replaced. It's pretty weathered. Hang on." She darts to her kitchen, her sweet ass dragging my focus, and comes back with a piece of paper. "I was thinking something like this."

I take the paper from her and look at the drawing. "You sketched this?"

She nods. "Impressed?"

"Very."

"You should be."

I can't help but smile. Beautiful and witty. A dangerous combination.

Like I said, trouble in a bikini, and I'd be wise to remember that.

I tug a business card from my back pocket and hand it to her. "My brother Sean will check it out and give you a quote."

She reads the print, then flicks the card against her hand. "Blue Bay Construction. Concise. To the point. I like that."

Yeah, and I like her.

Fuck me twice.

"Sean will find the right man for the job."

"Oh, I thought you—"

"Busy next door," I say, even though the job is almost done. "But if you want my opinion, I'd go with composite next time. The salt water is a bitch, and you'll end up replacing the wood in another ten years."

"Good plan. Thanks. I'll give your brother Sean a call, or maybe I'll stop in to see him. I have to run to town anyway." I turn to leave, and she says, "See you soon, Jamie."

Not if I fucking see her first.

KYLEE

I stand in the living room, unable to tear my eyes off Jamie Owens—his broad back and perfect ass, to be precise—as he exits through the screen door. He disappears around the corner, out of my line of sight and I suck in a breath to refill my collapsed lungs.

The guy is all rough and tough, so freaking sexy in a tool belt, my knees wobble and my damn ovaries are seconds from exploding. They sure as heck don't make them like that back in Atlanta, and once I go to work in Daddy's law firm come fall, the only men I'll face off against will be wearing suits and ties. Not that there is anything wrong with suits and ties, but shirtless in low-slung jeans and a tool belt, well, that trumps white-collar any day. Honest to God, Jamie is alpha male personified. The antithesis of Trevor Jackson, the suit-and-tie guy my father has been trying to set me up with for some time now. I went on a few dates at my father's insistence, but there was no chemistry, no connection, but my father is still pushing him on me—and Trevor has yet to let up. He wants what Dad wants.

Uh, hello, Dad, you strong-armed me into working at your

firm, but no way, no how will I allow you to force me into an arranged marriage. Not going to happen. Ever. Trevor was the one who told Dad about Blue Bay. He grew up in Atlanta, but apparently he and his family summered here every year when they were younger and still have a cottage on the ocean. I guess maybe he's hoping we can summer here together when we're married. Like hell.

As I think about my overbearing father and working in his office, under his thumb, it dampens my mood and kicks my arousal to the curb. I look around the gorgeous beachside mansion my father bought me—a consolation gift as far as I'm concerned—something to appease me after I agreed to go work for him instead of following my dreams.

Seriously, you'd think I had it all, right? A college degree: check. A position at Daddy's law firm come fall: check. A gorgeous house in Blue Bay to summer in: check. But what I —the obedient daughter of a very powerful man who controls my every move—don't have is a smoking hot, tattooed carpenter in my bed. I've had my whole life mapped out for me, and if I have to spend it in criminal law instead of pursuing a career in fashion design like I want, then just once I want to be bad, want to do something just for myself.

Like seduce the carpenter next door.

There's no denying the attraction between us. When he walked into my room and found me naked, need, want, and something dangerously dark flashed in those gorgeous green eyes of his. I've never seen eyes that color before. I'm guessing the two guys who came to my rescue are related, since they both have that same rare color.

Anyway, while there was a spark between Jamie and me, he did seem rather anxious to get out of my place. I hope he's not taken, because if I'm going to be bad this summer, I want to be bad with him. I'll have to do a little digging. He might not have a girl's name inked on his body, but that doesn't mean he's single. If he is, however, I'll need to find a way to entice him into my bed—a naughty way to get him to break that steely control he exudes.

I pull on a sundress, slip into a pair of sandals, and look at the business card again. I'm not exactly sure where Blue Bay Construction's home office is, but I'm heading to town, and since everyone here seems to know everyone, I'm sure someone can point me in the right direction.

Outside, I take another glance up and watch Jamie as he picks up a load of shingles. His big muscles bulge and I go all jittery inside. He seems lost in thought, a dreamer like me. I chuckle. Maybe we have more in common than I think. As if sensing my staring, he angles his head my way, and I give a finger wave. He doesn't wave back, instead he looks at me with those gorgeous, murderous eyes of his. Like he doesn't know whether to take me to bed or put me over his lap.

I wouldn't be opposed to either.

I climb into the car and back out of the driveway, leaving my cottage in my rearview mirror as I drive through the town. It's late May, and from what I understand, things don't really get under way here until the end of June or early July, once the kids are out of school. Since I was called to the bar last month, I decided to come early, get settled in, take some much-needed time to myself before the crowd rolls in.

I park my car at a metered spot and make my way to Benny's for groceries. This town is unlike any other I've ever been in. So quaint. It sort of reminds me of Lake Winnipesaukee in that old nineties movie, *What About Bob*, starring Bill Murray and Richard Dreyfuss. Yeah, old movies are a weakness of mine—scary ones too, although I usually end up hiding under my covers after watching them. How many times did my father berate me for my foolishness and overactive imagination? Thinking of my father reminds me that this town is a far cry from where I come from, and I actually really like it.

I walk along the streets, check out all the cute shops, and smile as I momentarily suspend reality and picture myself living in this town, my own specialty boutique full of designer clothes made by my hands. A car horn honks, and I'm jolted back to the present, but as I think of my designs, I consider Jamie's ink. The man does have talent. A hell of a lot of it, actually. Why did he leave his shop in New Orleans to pursue construction?

I have no idea why, but I wonder if he still has his equipment. If so, would he give me a tattoo? I laugh, and when someone passes by and looks at me strangely, I cover my mouth. I don't need anyone thinking a crazy lady just moved to town. But seriously, wouldn't a tattoo send Father Dearest over the edge. I'm not eighteen anymore. I'm twenty-six and if I want ink, I should damn well have ink. I open the door to Benny's as a naughty, delicious idea begins to form.

The irresistible scent of cinnamon and apple pie hits and my stomach grumbles. I wave to Benny Monroe as I grab a cart. I met him a few days ago when I stopped in to pick up a few necessities. I fill my basket and take it to the front to unload. Benny looks like the kind of man who knows everyone's business.

I pull the card Jamie gave me from my purse and show it to him. "You wouldn't happen to know where I could find Blue Bay Construction, would you?" He opens his mouth to speak, but closes it and smiles as someone shuffles in beside me.

"I'm headed there right now," a woman says, and when I turn, I find an elderly lady with those same green eyes looking up at me. "You can follow me."

"That would be wonderful, thank you."

She stares at me longer than is comfortable, like she's

trying to figure out who I am. "Where did you get the card?" she asks.

"Oh, Jamie Owens. He's doing work on a neighboring house."

"You're new in town."

It's a statement, not a question, but I answer anyway. "Yes, just bought a property on the water. I'm looking to have the deck replaced, which is why Jamie gave me this card."

She purses her lips and looks down for a moment, like she's remembering something from the past, then she says, "Well, I'm his Grandma Nellie, and I personally greet every newcomer to Blue Bay with a dinner invitation."

"That's so kind of you, but—"

Benny's chuckle has my words falling off. I turn to him and he has a gleam in his eyes—one that says, no way, no how am I getting out of Sunday dinner. Then again, maybe it won't be so bad. Maybe I can get a glimpse into Jamie's life and figure out if my naughty plan will actually work.

"You'll come this Sunday night," Grandma Nellie says.

I laugh. I've only just met her and in two days I'll be seated at her table. The people move fast in a town that moves slowly. "Okay." I nod toward the door. "Jamie told me to find Sean, and he'd give me a quote on the deck."

"Oh he did, did he? Didn't want to give you one himself?"

"No, he told me to check with Sean, and that Sean would find the right man for the job."

Her lips purse, and she goes quiet, like she's thinking of something. Her body language reminds me so much of Jamie, it's not funny.

"Interesting." I'm about to ask why that's interesting when Benny laughs again, and Grandma Nellie fires another question. "How long are you in town?"

My, my, for a little grandmother, she sure is a nosy one. "Until the end of the summer."

"That'll do. Follow me," she responds abruptly.

That'll do?

We both pay for our groceries, and I make a move to help with her bag. She swats me away and points a finger at me.

"Don't be fussing and treating me like an old lady who can't do things for herself."

I pull my hand back, and she struts past me, carrying her own bag. Alrighty then!

"See you later, Benny," she says and shifts the bag to open the door.

I grin at Benny and he just shakes his head, the look in his eyes warning that I'm about to go down the rabbit hole and never come out the same. Maybe I should heed it.

The bell over the door jingles, pulling my focus, and I decide nothing ventured, nothing gained. After playing by the rules for so long, I deserve a break from reality with hot carpenter guy—so I follow her out. I see a motorcycle and a big pickup truck parked outside and as she heads in that direction, I wonder which one she's driving. I chuckle to myself. She's not like any grandma I've ever known. I guess they grow them tough and sturdy in Blue Bay, and I'm also betting she played a major role in raising Jamie, considering he seems as obstinate as her and has the same mannerisms.

She hops into the big-ass truck, and I jump into my Lexus and follow her down the road until we're a little bit out of the town. She turns down a long driveway, and a big house looms in the distance. I park and hop from the vehicle.

Beneath the warm sun, I smooth my hair back and take in the massive homestead. "You have a beautiful home."

She smiles, and it's so warm and friendly I feel an instant camaraderie with her. "My grandfather built it when Blue Bay was a whaling community," she explains.

"You must have grown up in a big family."

"I did, and I also raised a lot of boys in that house."

"All boys?" I ask.

"Sons and grandsons." Her green eyes glisten. "I'm hoping for a great-granddaughter soon."

My throat dries. Dammit, I hope it's not Jamie she's talking about. I'm still holding out hope that he's available.

"This way." She leads me along a path and points to a door. "You'll find Sean in there, and don't forget, Sunday dinner, six sharp." I reach for the door handle when her voice stops me. "And just for the record, Jamie is the deck expert." She gestures with a nod toward her front deck. "He fixed that for me when he came home last year. It's good and sturdy. Just like him."

I angle my head. If I didn't know better, I'd think Grandma Nellie was doing a bit of matchmaking. Should I tell her I'm not interested in long-term and kids aren't on my horizon? As a lawyer who is going to work eighteen-hour days, no way would I bring a child into this world. Even though I barely saw my father growing up, he still managed to control my life, and I don't want to be an absent or controlling parent like him. Mom is gone now but she was no different, a busy district attorney, and too caught up in her position in society to be there for her kid. And of course I can't forget the fact that my past relationships have left me with a bad taste in my mouth. Apparently I'm a magnet for selfish jerks who are too focused on themselves and their own successes, most wanting to date me to get closer to Daddy. Ugh, I've yet to meet a man who wasn't self-centered or would even dream of putting my needs before his.

But before I can say any of those things, a big, slobbering Labrador retriever rounds the corner and darts toward me. I gasp, but when the animal starts licking me, I realize I'm not in any danger.

"Well hello there." I bend to pet the dog's head. I always did love animals, but they were messy and required a lot of attention, and with everyone working so hard, away for such long hours, I never thought it was fair to bring one home. Not that I thought my parents would ever let me while I was growing up.

"Scout, wait," someone yells, and when a girl around my age comes around the corner with a very big belly, I stand back up. "I'm sorry," she says and puts one hand on the wall as she gasps for breath. "I'm not as fast as I used to be, being twelve months pregnant and all, and Scout likes to run."

"Twelve months?"

She laughs. "Eight really, it just feels like twelve."

I laugh, and when I hear a screen door clang shut behind me, I turn to see a flash of Grandma Nellie's skirt as she enters her house.

"I see you met Gram," the girl says.

I nod. "She brought me here. I met her at Benny's and she told me to follow her."

Her eyebrows rise. "Oh, really?"

"I'm looking for Sean."

"Then you came to the right place." She angles her head and narrows her eyes. "Do I know you?"

I pet the dog again. "Do you walk Scout on the beach every morning?"

"I do."

She smiles at me and I instantly like her. I could use a friend in Blue Bay. "I thought I recognized you, too. I'm Kylee Jensen, just bought a cottage on the water."

"I'm Summer Owens. I'm married to the man you're looking for, and I'm your neighbor. Sean and I live a few doors down from you."

"You're married to Jamie's brother," I say, a statement, not a question.

Her eyes flash to me and open a little wider. "You know Jamie?"

"He's doing roof repair work on the cottage next to mine. When I asked about deck repairs, he gave me this card and told me to talk to Sean. He said Sean had the right man for the job."

She grins. "Oh he did, did he?"

Why is her reaction so much like Grandma Nellie's?

"Yeah, he told me I should use a composite. It's more permanent."

Summer opens the door to the office, her grin widening, and I can't help but think, *Foot, meet rabbit hole.*

"Well, come on in. Let's talk about permanent and see about getting the right man for that job."

Wait, she's still talking about my deck, right?

What the fuck is she doing here?

I'd given her Sean's card two days ago, and she's at Gram's for dinner already. Shit. I never should have let her drive out here. I should have just given her a damn quote on the deck myself and called in one of the guys to do the work before Sean had the chance to give the job to me, ignoring the fact that I told him I didn't want it. Fucker.

Leave it to Gram to invite her to dinner right after meeting her. But so help me God, if she tries to pair the two of us up, I'm fucking out of here. Ever since Sean and Summer got married, proving the Owens boys do have monogamy in them—well, some of us anyway—Gram has been trying to match us all up. She's damn determined to get a brood of great-grandkids. But she has to know I'd never, ever go for a girl like Kylee. Not that I know a lot about her. I don't need to. She's rich and pampered and that's enough for me. It should be enough for Gram, too.

"Hey," I grumble under my breath when I enter the kitchen to find Gram, Summer, and Kylee sipping on wine and whispering fuck-knows-what about fuck-knows-who. As long as it's not about me, we're good. All eyes turn to me.

"Jamie," Gram says. "Come here, sweet boy. Give your grandmother a hug."

Fuck, I wish she wouldn't call me that, especially in front of Kylee. I step up to her, but I'm full of dirt and grime from the roofing job, which Ryan and I just finished up an hour ago.

"I'm dirty, Gram."

As soon as those words leave my mouth, I hear Kylee suck in a fast breath. I look over Gram's head, my gaze going to hers, and when I spot big blue eyes moving over my body, there is a part of me that would like to show the girl next door just how dirty I am—just how sweet I'm not, despite what Gram thinks. I clear my throat and give Gram a peck on the cheek.

"What time is dinner? I need to shower."

"Me too," Jared, one of the twins, says, coming in behind me looking like he had a hell of a day too. His boots scruff the floor then come to a resounding halt when he sees Kylee, and it takes every ounce of strength I possess not to shift and put my body in between them to cut off his line of vision. Jared will fuck anything that moves, and if he thinks for one minute I'm letting him near Kylee, he can forget it.

Jesus Christ, what am I even thinking?

Oh, I don't know, maybe that deep down I want her in my bed.

Fuck that.

"I don't think we've met," Jared says.

I clench down, and Gram says, "Everything okay, Jamie?"

"Fine," I bite out.

Ignoring me, Jared walks up to Kylee. "I'm Jared, and we couldn't have met because I'd never forget a girl like you."

"Real fucking original," I mumble under my breath.

Gram does the introduction, and I lean against the door-jamb, trying to ignore the way Summer is smirking at me, like she fucking knows what's going on inside my head—and inside my pants. I love my sister-in-law, I really do, but she needs to stay the hell out of my business.

"Of course you don't need an introduction, Jamie," Gram says. "Kylee told me you two met at the beach, and that's how I came to know her."

Well done, dude.

I make a move to go, but my feet still when Gram says, "Jared, why don't you refill Kylee's wine glass and give her a tour of the property. Take her down to the lake. It's so pretty this time of night. Supper will be a little while yet."

"Sure," Jared says and grabs the bottle to refill Kylee's glass.

"Not too much. I'm a lightweight," Kylee says.

"No worries. If you have too much, I'll see to it that you get home safely."

I'm going to fucking kill him.

The screen door bangs shut as Jared leads her outside, and I don't stick around to let Gram or Summer see the shit storm going on inside me. I make my way upstairs, tugging my grimy shirt off as I go, and step into the bathroom. Because I'm a goddamn masochist, I step up to the window in time to see Jared put his hand around Kylee's back and carefully lead her out to the wharf.

I kick off my pants and turn on the water. I should probably take a cold shower. No one needs to see my boner at the dinner table. I climb in, grab the soap, and lather up. My cock refuses to cooperate and continues to swell as I think of Kylee. I grip the base and give a hard tug. Fuck, that feels good. Unable to help myself, I close my eyes, envision Kylee in here with me. What I'd do to bend her over the edge and drive my cock into her. I keep stroking as I picture her spread wide open for me, and it doesn't take long before I'm shooting a load off into the stream of water. Good, that should help clear my head and get me through a meal unscathed.

I stay under the spray longer, using up all the hot water until it turns colder. A little smile of satisfaction curls my lips. Jared needs a shower too. It will be a cold one. Maybe that will help him cool down and stop eye fucking Kylee. He's not the man for her.

Neither am I.

I pull a towel out from the cabinet, knot it around my waist, and pick my clothes up off the floor. My fingers tighten around the doorknob and I give myself a quick lecture to keep my shit together, then pull the door open. When I find a very surprised, very sexy Kylee on the other side, my cock swells, despite having just jacked off in the shower.

What the fuck?

Her gaze slowly rolls over me, and her cheeks turn a pretty shade of pink. Damn, that shade of pink is fast becoming my favorite color, and it makes me want to explore the rest of her body in search of more pink sweetness.

"We need to stop meeting like this," she says, her voice breathless.

"I guess we're even now."

"Not quite."

My towel is tenting but it's too late to conceal my erection. Nope, it's right out there in the world for all to see what Kylee Jensen does to me. "No?"

"You saw me naked."

Son of a bitch. Walk away dude. Don't let this go any farther.

I brace one arm on the doorjamb above my head. "You want to see me naked, Kylee?" I taste her name on my tongue, savor it, wonder how it will sound when I'm coming inside her. My cock grows another inch.

Dark lashes flash over blue eyes. "I never said that."

"So that's a no?"

She goes quiet for a moment, her chest rising and falling. The low neckline of her sundress showcases her cleavage, and it takes everything in me to keep my eyes from straying. My hand grips the dirty clothes harder, anything to keep it occupied.

"I never said that either," she says, her voice so low I have to strain to hear it.

Despite my best interests, I step in to her until our bodies are touching, my cock pressed against her stomach, letting her know the effect she has on me. Stupid move on my part, for sure. I slide my hand around her neck, under her long hair, and splay my fingers as I wet my parched lips. This girl is looking for trouble, and if I don't get my shit together, she's soon going to find it.

"What are you doing, Kylee?"

I hear a noise on the steps and let her go. She falters slightly as my brother Tyler comes racing up the stairs and into the hall. "Jared is showering downstairs," she says, pulling herself together in Ty's presence so quickly it impresses me. "So Gram told me to come up here and get washed up for dinner. I guess she thought you were done with your shower."

"I'm done." I step around her and wave my hand for her to enter.

"Thanks," she says and disappears inside.

"What's up bro," Ty says, breezing past me to go to his room.

"Nothing."

He spins. "Whoa, what the fuck is wrong with you, man?"

"Not a goddamn thing." I grumble and step into my room, slamming the door shut as sexual frustration builds inside me. I will not, under any circumstances, put my hands on her again. One touch of her body and I was ready to forget that pampered women like her, ones seeking danger from the bad boy on the wrong side of the tracks, are nothing but trouble for me.

I pull on a pair of clean jeans and a T-shirt and meet the family downstairs. By the time I enter the kitchen, all four of my brothers and three cousins are there, and it makes me happy to see Gram so thrilled to be cooking for the army known as the Owens boys. This old homestead must have been lonely for her when we all took off to find our own paths in life. It's crazy to think it took Dad's death last year to bring us all back together again. He was a hard-ass son of a bitch, but I sure do miss the guy. He hated that I was a dreamer, and I thought he was going to beat the living shit out of me after I was charged with rape. I hated that he didn't believe me, or believe in me, or even care that I had aspirations to be a tattoo artist. *Only an idiot would put ink under their skin.* That hurt like a son of a bitch, but it's a life lesson I'll never forget. Christ, he'd probably roll over in his grave if he knew I was opening my own shop here in Blue Bay. He never supported anything I did.

Pushing those dark thoughts to the recess of my mind where they belong, I grab a big bowl of mashed potatoes and set it on the long oaken table in the dining room. Gram and Kylee come in behind me and add the pot roast, carrots, turnips, and parsnips. There is enough food to feed an army and then some.

"Where should I sit?" Kylee asks.

"Right here," Jared says, tapping the seat beside him. *My fucking seat.* The bastard is messing with me. Then again, how could he know how much I want Kylee Jensen all to myself?

"Good idea, Jared," Gram says, and I turn to her.

"You can sit next to me, sweet boy," she says.

Everyone files in and we all take our seats. Soon enough the talk turns to work, and I try to ignore Kylee across from me, try to ignore my swelling cock as she slides her fork into her mouth and licks her lips in delight. It takes every ounce of strength I possess not to grab her, take her to my room, and force her to her knees so I can put my cock in that lush mouth of hers.

"Isn't that right, Jamie?"

"What?" I ask, looking up from the mashed potatoes that I've been making railroads in with my fork.

"The composite for Kylee's deck is supposed to arrive tomorrow, right?" Sean repeats.

"Yeah."

"It shouldn't be too much work to tear the old deck down. I have a bin set to arrive tomorrow for the debris," Sean explains.

Why the hell did he give the job to me?

"You need any help with that job?" Jared asks as he smiles at Kylee. "I'm almost done on the Baxter expansion. Just another week or two."

"No," I say quickly. Too fucking quickly, considering every pair of eyes has suddenly turned my way. "The deck is a hazard and needs to be done right away. I checked it out myself. Isn't that right Kylee?"

"That's right. It's a dilapidated mess and a hazard," she agrees and I hope that takes the attention off me. Ryan, though, that bastard needs to stop smirking at me before I take him outside and wipe it off his face myself.

"Enough work talk," Gram says and turns to Kylee.

"What do you do, child?"

"I'm a lawyer," Kylee says quietly, like the word tastes sour on her tongue.

"A lawyer," Gram exclaims and claps her hands. "How impressive."

Impressive? Yeah, I guess. Not that I have a love for lawyers, and truthfully, that's the last thing I expected her to say, and all the more reason to stay away from her. When I was arrested I learned just how manipulative lawyers could be. They had far too many tricks up their sleeves and spouted nothing but legal jargon from their sharp mouths. My gaze goes to Kylee's mouth again, her soft pink lips specifically. I can think of other ways to put that mouth of hers to work.

On that note, I scoop a forkful of potatoes, chew, then say, "I thought you designed clothes or something."

Her eyes go wide, but then something wistful, something sad, moves across her face. "I do," she says, her brow pulling together. "How . . . oh, you must have seen my bedroom."

"What were you doing in her bedroom?" Jacob, the other twin, asks, his dimples spreading as he wiggles his eyebrows at me.

"I screamed when I found a spider in my bedroom, and Jamie and Ryan came running to my rescue." She grins at Gram. "They're both sweet boys."

Before one of my asshole brothers or cousins comes back with a smart-ass comment, Summer turns to look at the dress Kylee is wearing, her mouth agape. "You design clothes?"

Kylee shrugs like it's nothing but I get the sense that it's everything. She plucks at her dress, a vulnerability about her that sucks the air from my lungs quicker than one of Ty's rear naked chokeholds.

"It's a hobby," she says quietly. "My designs aren't good enough to sell."

Whoever the fuck told her that needs a beat-down. Shit, man, I shouldn't feel so protective of her, but I hate the hurt look on her face.

"My God, you're kidding me?" Summer bursts out. "This is gorgeous. I was admiring your dress earlier. They're definitely good enough to sell. Better than good enough. They're great."

She smiles at Summer, but beneath it there's a sadness,

like she really doesn't believe in her talent. I know the feeling. My brothers believed in me, but there was really only one man's approval I wanted, and he hated that I was a dreamer.

Tattooing isn't a man's job, construction is. Jesus, he was such a hard-ass prick, but I miss him like fuck.

"Like I said, it's a hobby."

Gram blinks up at me. "You're an artist, like my sweet boy here."

Kylee lets loose a little breath. "I'm not really an artist," she says. "And I won't have much time for it, once I begin practicing in September."

Summer gasps and puts her hand on her stomach. "This one," she says and turns to Tyler. "With a kick like that, I think this one is going to give you a run for your money, Ty."

Ty laughs. "Future MMA fighter."

"Not if I have anything to do with it," Summer says. "This one's going to be our next president. No one is punching my baby."

"He'll be whatever he wants to be," Sean says, and Summer nods.

"You're right. I'm not going to force him or her into doing a job they don't want."

Kylee looks down at her plate, her brow furrowed like she totally gets what Summer is saying.

"But I'm sure he or she will *want* to be president. I mean who wouldn't, right?" Summer adds with a wink.

"Not me," Tyler says and when the rest of the guys join in, everyone laughs. Summer winces when the baby kicks again. She reaches for Kylee's hand, and Kylee's eyes go wide when Summer asks, "Want to feel?" Before Kylee can answer, Summer takes her hand and puts it on her stomach.

"Oh, my God," Kylee says laughing. "Mrs. Owens, I'm not sure you're getting that girl. I think this one is going to be in the NFL."

"Call me Gram," she says with a wave of her hand. "And girls play football too. And if it's not a girl, we'll have to keep trying," Gram says and I don't miss the look she slides me. Jesus. "Oh, that reminds me. Summer, we need to head to Hope Falls to pick up your new crib tomorrow."

"Why don't you come along, Kylee?" Summer suggests. "They have a Starbucks in Hope Falls."

Jesus Christ, look at them all, bonding with the new girl.

"You know you shouldn't be drinking that," Sean says, and puts his arm around his wife's back.

"It's my one and only weakness, Sean. Besides, it's basically milk."

He arches a brow. "Your one and only weakness?" he asks.

She kisses him and grins. "Well, maybe not my one and only."

"Get a room," Jared says, and everyone laughs. Everyone except me. Nope, not laughing at all. I'm envisioning Kylee and me alone in a room, bare naked, and all the things I want to do to her. My cock thickens and I mentally marshal it back into submission.

On that note, I push back from the table, needing to get to my shop. "Thanks for dinner, Gram. It was great as always, but I have to get to work if I want the shop to be ready for the grand opening next month. I still have a lot of cleaning and painting to do."

Gram takes a sip of her tea. "No dessert?"

"He doesn't need it," Tyler says. "He's getting a little soft around the middle."

I glare at Tyler, my kid brother, the tough-as-nails cage fighter, and take in his smirk. "Want to take this outside? Let me show you I'm still your big brother."

"Yeah, around the middle." He laughs and adds, "I wouldn't want to embarrass you in front of our new friend."

Kylee smiles at that. "It's okay, I don't embarrass easily."

I call bullshit. I saw her blush. She definitely embarrasses easily and I'd give my left nut just to see her cheeks turn that pretty shade of pink again.

Summer pats Kylee's hand. "Don't worry, they're always like this. Too much testosterone in one room." She rubs her belly. "We need more girls in the family. To even things out."

"I'm not getting any younger, you know," Gram says. "I want my great-grandkids now while I can enjoy them."

We all groan and shake our heads. "Don't be out too late," Sean says. "You start on Kylee's deck tomorrow."

Lucky fucking me.

I was hoping to avoid her but now have no choice but to see her every goddamn day. "Yeah, I know," I say and take my plate to the kitchen before I step outside. I would have stayed to help with clean-up, but Gram hates us guys in her space. The warm air falls over me, and I breathe past the tightness in my throat. I hop on my bike and clear my head on my way to my small shop. I'd love to expand it someday, break down the south wall and add a new room. Ryan wants to learn the business, and once I get things up and running I plan to bring him on board and teach him. Perhaps if I make this place successful, I can prove there is more to me. Maybe then someone might believe in me. What the fuck am I talking about? I don't give two shits what anyone outside of the family thinks of me. But I'm getting ahead of myself. I've not even opened my doors yet, and I need to get the place cleaned up and in working order before I even think about sinking money I don't have into an expansion.

I kill the ignition on my bike, hop off, and unlock the door. The first thing I do is turn on the radio. Some old song comes on but I don't mind. I kind of dig the older music. I make my way to the bathroom to wash my hands before I start laying out the cloths to cover the furniture, then grab a cold beer from the fridge. I crack it and turn when I hear someone coming in behind me.

"I'm not op . . ." my voice falls off and my heart stalls when I see Kylee walking into the place like she owns it—and like she's looking for trouble.

"Hey, sweet boy," she says, and a growl catches in my throat as she runs her fingers over my things, flips the pages on my sketch book, and steps up to my reclining leather tattoo chair.

"What are you doing here?" I ask, my voice rough with arousal as her scent fills the small place.

"Well I was thinking about our tattoo conversation the other day."

"What about it?"

"I thought you could . . ." She slides into the chair, opens her legs, and says, "Ink me."

Kill me.

Fucking.

Now.

"I'm not inking you," he says through gritted teeth, his hands at his side, one gripping a bottle of beer and swinging it idly. He might be trying to pull off casual, but damn, he's coiled tighter than a class of law students awaiting news on their bar exams.

"Why not?"

The muscles along his jaw ripple and his eyes go dark, murderous, like he's fighting some kind of internal battle. "You were drinking at Gram's. I don't ink anyone who's consumed alcohol."

I wave my hand. "I had a glass of wine, Jamie. I hardly call that drinking."

"You had two glasses. Jared filled your glass before he took you down to the lake, remember?"

"Oh, right. I didn't realize you were keeping track. Still, I've had a meal since then, and I drove here. I'm not under the influence at all."

Nope, not at all, and the only thing I want to be under is *him*. But I'm guessing he knows that by now. Heck, he probably knew it the second I asked him if he wanted a drink after walking in on me naked.

He steps up to me, his Adam's apple bobbing like it's going down for the third count, and when I catch his scent, a mix of leather and hot, hard man, heat trickles through me. I take in the hardness in his eyes as he glares at me and suddenly I'm not so sure this is my brightest moment. I'm not used to rough and tough guys like him, ones who looks like they're going to eat me alive. Every instinct I possess tells me Jamie Owens is not a guy one should ever toy with—like I'm doing right now.

Suddenly skittish, I grip the sides of the chairs, about to get up, run far away from this man and the dangers he exudes, when he puts his legs on either side of my chair to cage me in place. His bottle hits the table beside me with a thud and my panicky heart races faster.

"Won't Daddy get upset?" He angles his head, his eyes moving over my face like he can see right through me. "Or maybe that's the point."

"I'm a grown woman," I say, going on the defense even though there is a sexual storm raging inside me. "I can do what I want."

"If you really want a tattoo, I'll give you one." His gaze leaves my mouth, travels leisurely down my body, and I squirm under his heated glare. He touches me, the pads of his thumb rough on my arm as he slides his hand downward, sending scorching heat through my veins. "But I'm not so sure that's why you're really here," he says, his voice deeper, darker.

"It is." Hot and needy from his touch, I stroke my pinned thighs. He widens his legs to let me inch mine open. "I want one right here," I say, naked lust overcoming my concerns and urging me on.

"Are you sure it's a *tattoo* you want on your thigh?"

Oh, God, when he looks at me like that, I can barely think. "I . . . uh . . ."

He grips my dress, drags it up my legs slowly, until my thighs are exposed. "Or maybe it's something else you want between your legs."

Oh. My. God.

"Like . . ." I begin, my ability to string a coherent sentence together abandoning me. "Like . . . what?"

I suck in a breath, but can't fill my lungs when he leans forward. "Like this." He brushes his rough tongue over my inner thigh and the world closes in on me.

"Jamie," I say, my body quaking from head to toe as his heat penetrates my skin and turns me into a quivering mess. He pulls back and I instantly miss the warmth of his mouth, the way the scruff on his chin chafes my flesh. God, I want him to use me, leave my body sore and abraded come morning.

"Yeah?" he asks, his deep voice rumbling through me as he grips my legs and widens them even more.

"I . . . I want . . ."

"What do you want?" he asks.

"You're right. I want your tongue," I say, shocking myself with my boldness, but it's useless to pretend otherwise. I came here for sex, and there isn't a damn thing wrong with two consenting adults having a little fun, no strings. Right? I mean, as long as we both know the score, where's the harm?

"What else do you want?" He lifts my dress higher, until my lace panties are exposed, and when he sucks in a fast breath it does something to me, makes me feel even more brazen, empowered.

"I want your tongue, your mouth, your fingers and . . ." I pause and lean forward, cupping his erection in my hand. "Your cock," I whisper, outing myself for the needy girl I am, one who hasn't been touched in far too long.

A shadow of a smile plays on his lips. "The girl wants a lot."

"Did the girl come to the right place?" Instead of answering, he runs his fingers along the band on my panties, brushing the backs of his fingers over my pubis. I quake beneath his touch as sexual tension hangs heavy. "What . . . what does the boy want?" I ask and he grins.

"The boy wants a lot too."

"Tell me," I whisper.

"I'd rather show you."

He presses his mouth to my sex, licking me though my panties. Oh, yeah, showing is way better than telling. Words are totally overrated.

I flush hotly. "Yes, please," I murmur and lift my hips, eager for so much more as his soft chuckle vibrates through me. My clit swells, and desperate to feel him, I reach out and put my hand on his chest, feel his fast heartbeat through his T-shirt, one that is preventing me from seeing his gorgeous body. Damn I hate that shirt. I grip it, tug at it, and he reaches behind his head and peels it off. It's such a sexy guy move, my pulse pounds double-time and I resist the urge to pinch myself. If this isn't really happening, I don't want to know. No, I want to live in the fantasy of bad boy Jamie for a few more hours.

"The girl wants this too?" he asks.

I take in the old scars on his body, the ones the tattoos can't cover. He even has one on his jawline, in the shape of an eagle, I think. I suddenly want to hurt whoever did this to him. But those thoughts are for a later time when I'm not squirming beneath him, a hot needy mess of desire.

"Yes, the girl wants this too," I say. I shift, and lift my sundress over my head, tossing it to the floor next to his shirt. He gazes at me, takes in my near-nakedness, then zeroes in on my lace bra. My nipples pucker painfully and poke through the material. "Does the boy want these?"

He wets his bottom lip, like he can already taste me. "He does," he says, a grin tugging at the corners of his mouth, and I love this little game we're playing.

But then his jaw clenches and his eyes go serious, almost feral. "Just for the record, I'm not as sweet as Gram thinks I am. I've wanted to bend you over and fuck you since the first time I laid eyes on you. You should probably know that before we go any farther."

"Sweet is overrated," I say and wiggle my ass in encouragement, eager for him to do just that. The green in his eyes deepens as he slides his hand around my head, roughly bringing my lips to his.

"Does the girl know what she's getting herself into?" he murmurs into my mouth, as we exchange hot, heated kisses that burn through my blood and zap my brain cells.

Not really.

"Yes," I say and widen my legs in a silent invitation. "Does the boy know what he's getting . . . *into?*" I tease, but he goes still at my playful words, a dark shadow ghosting even darker eyes. Oh, God, is he having second thoughts? I sure as hell hope not, because if he stops now, I think I might go up in flames and rain down in a bed of ash.

He shakes his head, and his too-long hair falls into his eyes. "I don't . . . I can't . . ."

Understanding dawns quickly as his body tightens. He told me he wanted me sexually, but some part of him must think I want more. "Just one night," I say addressing his worries. "No strings." I reach for him to pull his mouth back to mine, wanting to feel what's stirring between his legs again. I touch his body, brush my lips over his, tasting beer from a mouth that had just been between my legs—and wanting it there again, sans panties.

A change comes over him—an animal unleashed—and his lips crash over mine with a ferocity that frightens me as much as it excites me.

His tongue pushes into my mouth, tasting deeply as he presses his solid body over mine, his cock so hard and big against my stomach, I think I won the man lottery. With no effort he pulls me forward, unclasps my bra with an ease I don't want to think too much about, and drags the material from my body. My breasts are small, not one of my more flattering features, but holy God, the way he's gazing at me makes me feel like I have the nicest body in the world.

"Perfect," he murmurs quietly as he runs his palm along the underside of my breast. His touch is soft but his hard calluses caress me roughly. The combination is mind-blowingly delicious, and I'm hooked. He repositions himself between my legs and presses hot, open-mouthed kisses to my stomach as he crawls back up my body. He takes another second to look over my naked flesh, grips my rib cage beneath my breasts, and brushes his thumbs over my nipples.

"These," he begins, a raw ache of lust in his voice. "The boy likes these, and he needs to spend a whole lot of time with them." He licks my nipples, a lazy caress that belies the hungry heat in his gaze, then pulls the pebbled nub into his mouth. He cups one breast and kneads it, his hot mouth working magic on the other. He clenches down on my nipple. Hard. So hard, in fact, I feel the pull all the way to my sex.

I tremble from head to toe, run my fingers through his hair, and arch into him. "That feels so good," I murmur. I push his hair from his face and glance down at him, wanting to watch his mouth on my body. God, not only has his touch turned me into an addict, now I'm a voyeur, too?

I groan in bliss as he greedily takes my other nipple into his mouth and alternates between licking, sucking, and nibbling. Good God, if he keeps it up, I just might climax, and I've never climaxed from nipple stimulation before. Then again, I'm doing a lot of things I've never done before, all because of this hot man between my legs.

His mouth leaves my breasts and he kisses a path downward, but stops and inhales, like he's breathing me in, filling his lungs with my scent. He steals another glance up at me, the hungry look in his eyes so potent, air leaves my lungs in a whoosh. I love his rawness, the way his green eyes display his deep-seated need, his lack of inhibitions.

A loud growl rumbles in his throat and he nips at my panties, tugging them lower on my hips. I lift for him, so damn eager he chuckles at my enthusiasm. But it doesn't make me feel silly. No, it makes me feel sexy and desired. Like I'm finally in the right hands. Everything in this man's touch makes me feel alive, wanted . . . uninhibited. Truthfully, I might have only had two drinks earlier, but my vision is wobbly, drunk on the man before me. Too bad I only asked for one night. Then again, with a man like him, asking for more could only lead to trouble.

He stands, shimmies my panties to my ankles, and tugs them off. The air around me grows thin as he sucks in a deep breath and lets it out slowly. "You are incredible," he murmurs, his fingers biting into my thighs as he spreads them wider. His eyes simmer with fierceness—a controlled fire— and I'm hyperaware of his power, the wildness he's working to tame. But I want him wild. I want him to let go and take full possession of me—the way he needs—the way I need.

When have I ever felt such need?

I sit up and press my mouth to his chest. I kiss him, run my tongue over his taut nipples, and his growl urges me on. His hands grip my hair and tug, but I don't inch back. Instead, I open his pants and slide my hand inside. I stroke his huge cock, dip into the liquid pooling on his crown, and use it for lubrication.

"Jesus fuck," he growls and I smile. I slide from the seat and go down on my knees in front of him. His hands clench my hair as I tug his jeans down to free his gorgeous cock.

"Mmm," I whisper and caress the long length of him. "So nice." I lean into him, and his crown hits the back of my throat. He's too damn big for me to take all of him in. That's not going to stop me from trying, though.

His hips jerk forward, and I stretch my jaw to accommodate his girth. My pulse is thumping now, pounding so hard against my neck, it's getting harder and harder to breathe. Then again, it could be the big cock in my mouth that's cutting off my air supply. But I don't care. I take him deeper into my throat and his heated curses curl around me and fill me with hunger.

"Fuck, Kylee," he growls and I love the way my name sounds on his tongue when he's lost in lust. My sex tightens with impatience, desperate to be filled, but I don't want to stop what I'm doing. I want to taste his cum, want him to shoot down my throat, fill me completely. I work my mouth quicker and cup his balls. They tighten into his body and I know he's close to releasing. I whimper, waiting for him to do just that, but he seems to have other ideas.

He grips my shoulders and pulls me to him. His eyes are inflamed, full of urgent need when they reach mine. He touches my face, my collarbone, my breasts, as his knee slides between my legs. He pulls me down onto his thigh and I ride it, rubbing my wet pussy all over him. His hot fingers, rough and restless, roam my quivering body and leave me burned and branded. He kisses me, fast, fevered . . . filthy . . . and I love every second of it. I've always been a good girl, but there is something so delicious naughty—almost taboo—in the way we're making out in his tattoo shop. How will I ever go back to white-collar after a night with him?

A dark, tortured sound rumbles in his throat, as I rub

myself on his thigh. I've never been so free before, so blatantly open and needy. God, I've always performed with a certain decorum and wouldn't dare act this way with any of the guys I've been with. But not only does Jamie seem to like me like this, he's encouraging my naughty behavior.

Thank you, Jamie.

"I need to taste you," he growls and pushes on my shoulders until I'm on the chair again. His nostrils flare as his heated gaze drinks me in. He touches my thigh, grips it hard. "I need my tongue inside you when you come for me."

Yes, please . . .

His fingers bite into my skin hard enough to leave a bruise as he spreads my legs wide. He bends my knees and pushes on my legs until they're pressed against my sides. As he opens me to him completely, his eyes meet mine. I take in his dilated pupils surrounded by a dark stormy sea of green.

Breathless, I stare at him, and his hair falls forward as he dips his head, presses his mouth to my sex. Oh, God. My hips rise up to meet his mouth as his tongue sears my aching clit. He draws slow circles around it, stirring the need building inside me. A sound rises from the depths of my throat as I reach out and grip his head. He continues to feast on me, kissing my sex deeply as he plucks at my clit. The dual assault is the most amazing thing I've ever felt. Did it get better than this? He pushes a finger inside me as his other hand slides up my body to cup my breast. He strokes my nipple roughly, and I moan. I guess I was wrong. It did get better. His mouth on my clit, a finger inside me, and a hand on my breast—the perfect trifecta. Heat flashes inside me, making me light-headed. Lost in ecstasy, I cry out beneath his invading mouth as he slides a finger in and out of me. I'm so wet and slick, so ready to come apart my body shudders almost violently.

"I want you to come in my mouth," he whispers from between my legs. "I want your taste on my tongue for the rest of the night, then I'm going to flip you over and ride the fuck out of you."

His sinful words nearly send me over the edge. Every muscle in my body clenches, my flesh tightening as he traces my clit with his thumb. He grins like he can read my thoughts. Guys like him don't ask for what they want, they take it, but everything in his expression tells me he's going to give it as good as he's getting it. I swallow a moan of excitement.

"Does the girl want that?"

"Yes," I cry out as he slides another finger inside me, like he knows exactly what it's going to take to push me over the precipice. Holy hell, I've never felt so gloriously full before—so completely done for. A pleasure so intense the room fades in on me races through my body. "Jamie," I cry out, my sex clenching around his invading fingers. "Yes, Jamie . . . yes . . . just like that. Don't . . . stop."

I close my eyes, completely lost in euphoria, and he stays between my legs, lapping at me as I ride out the crashing waves. When I finally stop, he slides up my body, his breath like hot steam on my skin.

He kisses my nipples, then inches back. I reach for him, but he grips my hips, and in a move so fast it takes me by surprise, he flips me over.

"Fuck yeah," he says and slides a big hot palm over my ass. He gives it a small slap and I yelp. His hand slides up my back and he grips my hair, and he gives a little tug as his other hand slides under my stomach to lift me for him. I lay there, open and vulnerable, my ass in the air. I should be embarrassed by the way he's displaying me, but I'm not and when I hear his sharp moan, my mind goes blank, wanting only whatever it is he's going to give me.

I hear a drawer open, then a foil crinkle. Yes, condom! I was so lost in him, I'd almost forgotten. At least one of us has enough wits to think about protection. He repositions me on the seat, drags me lower until his cock is lined up with my sex. He leans over me, adjusting his erection, and slides it along the crevice of my ass. Oh, God, I hope he's not planning to take me like that. My worries dissolve when he dips his crown into my slick heat, offering me a taste of things to come.

"Yes, Jamie," I say, and his grip on my hair tightens. "The girl wants your cock."

He goes still for a second, and then in one thrust enters me, pushing the air from my lungs as he stuffs me wholly. I gasp, and he bucks, hot and slick, moving his hard flesh inside me, a deep penetration that reaches places no man has ever reached before. Rough and rugged, he takes me hard, his cock stretching me wide. I move with him, match each thrust. His hips bang against my ass as he pistons into me, and sensations grip me hard, take hold, own me completely.

A pleasure so intense it almost hurts engulfs me. I'm drowning. Suffocating. Unable to surface as crashing waves keep pulling me under, deeper into the depths of desire. This is too much. He's too much. I need him to stop almost as much as I need him to continue.

"Jamie," I cry out, panting, gulping for air, but unable to find any.

He puts his arms around me and pulls me back up to his body. His heart pounds against my back as I keep orgasming around his hard cock. "I've got you," he whispers into my ear, his lips wet against my lobe. True to his word, he secures me against his hard body as I continue to shatter around him, and when the waves finally stop crashing, and I'm able to surface for air, he loosens his hold, but doesn't stop touching me.

What the hell was that?

Jamie Owens.

I've always been with safe guys, not bad boys who fuck like wild animals—or maybe it's just Jamie who fucks like that. I had no idea what I was missing out on. But my thoughts dissolve because he's rocking into me again, fucking me hard, a brutal pounding that taunts my sex again and almost has me pleading to the gods. He repositions, placing one hand on my hip for leverage, the other on my breast. He's grunting, groaning, and reaching a frenzied pace that has my clit throbbing double-time. With little finesse he pinches my nipple, and I start coming again. My God, sex with this man is insane. He pulls me up again, his cock still deep inside me as hot lips move to the back of my neck, each labored breath sending heated shivers over my skin.

His fingers go to my clit as he slides almost all the way out, and I move against his hand and rear back, seeking more. Sex with him is too much, yet not near enough. I know that doesn't make sense, but my body has never burned so deeply before. He shoves into me, spearing me hard, and I groan. A little nudge to my shoulders has me going back down onto my hands and knees. He moves, rocks into me, his body seeking release, each pump designed to take him where he needs to go.

Needing to help him get there and loving the way he's losing control, I tighten my sex muscles and he growls, throws his head back, and lets go high inside me. Each hard pulse nurtures my orgasm, and my hot release drips down my thighs. His moan, a low desperate needy sound, fills the air, and I shut my eyes against the world, wanting only to exist in this fantasy one, with this man, for just a little bit longer.

Big hands grip my waist and pick me up. He turns me, settles me on the seat, and rests his forehead against mine. I slacken against him as we breathe together for a long time. He places a kiss on my mouth so gentle, so tender, and so deeply intimate, it takes me by surprise.

"The girl is good?" he asks and pulls me to him until our bodies are meshed. "Or does she need something else?"

I slide my arms around his back, and run my hands over his taut muscles. His cock grows against my stomach as I touch him, and I can't believe he's ready to go again.

"*Hard* to say," I answer. I know we don't have a future, but we do have tonight, and I plan to take full advantage of that —of him.

He chuckles, and the sound vibrates through me. "*Hard* indeed," he murmurs as his lips close over mine.

The soft hums drifting outside through the open cottage window reach my ears and my body instantly hardens. Listing to Kylee's sweet noises is fucking with my hard-earned focus. Not great for a guy who's about to use a circular saw.

Kylee.

Sweet Kylee who sucked my cock so nicely and tasted like heaven on my tongue. My dick twitches and throbs in remembrance. She gave her body over to me last night, mine to do with as I pleased, and when she came so damn hard for me, so many times, it totally blew my fucking mind. I've never seen a woman come and come and come like that before. What I'd do to make it happen again . . .

Standing on her back deck, under the morning sun, I turn on the saw and cut into the wood, channeling the heat brewing in my body into removing the structure from the house. But Jesus, it's hard to concentrate with her mere feet away making sexy bedroom noises that make me want to bend her over and drive my dick into her again. Except, after an incredible night with her, I swore to fucking God to keep my hands to myself from here on out. She asked for one night, and that's all this can be. She's trouble with a capital T, and I'm not interested in getting back into her panties anyway. *Fucking liar.* Seriously though, once was enough. Or at least it should have been, goddammit.

Okay, enough of this shit.

I set the saw down, wipe my brow with the back of my hand, and open the screen door to put a stop to her humming. I follow the sound, and when I round the corner and come to the first bedroom to see her swaying her hips as she hums, the fight to keep my distance instantly goes out of me. Just like that. What a goddamn motherfucking weak-ass son of a bitch I am. But she's so fucking beautiful, and I can't help but want her again. As if sensing me behind her she turns, and her eyes go wide.

"I didn't hear you come in."

I glance at her lush mouth. Fuck, when she wrapped those sweet lips around my cock, I could hear the damn angels singing, and I'm not even a religious guy.

Get it together, dude. It was a one-night thing.

"You were humming," I say through clenched teeth.

She smiles at me, a smile so sexy and sweet my dick aches in my pants. "I hum when I'm working," she says, and it's all I can do not to tell her to continue so I can lose myself in the soft warmth of her voice. But that's the last thing I want.

My gaze goes from her to the marked-up sketch pad on a drafting board under the window. I stiffen when I see her designs. She's talented, but why the fuck is she designing baby clothes. I hope she's not thinking we're . . .

"Oh," she says quickly, obviously picking up on my unease. "I thought I'd make something for Summer's baby. Since she doesn't know if she's having a boy or a girl, I thought I'd make one of each. An original design." She holds the sketch pad up, and I take in the outfits she's sketching. "Do you think she'll like it?" She frowns and adds, "Do you think it's good enough?"

Good enough?

Why the hell wouldn't she think it was good enough?

"I just really wanted to do something nice for her. She's been so nice to me."

My heart squeezes at her thoughtfulness, and unable to ignore the heat sparking between us, I make quick work of the distance keeping me from her. As I crowd her, invade her private space, her breathing changes, becomes deeper. I touch her face, run my fingers over her cheek. "I think she'll love it," I say. I slide my hand around her neck and dip my head. She's looking up at me, her eyes big, her breath warm on my face. I shouldn't be doing this, but my traitorous fucking cock refuses to cooperate. All it can think about is sliding back into her wet heat.

"Kylee," I murmur.

"Yeah." She leans into me and parts her lips, her look so sweet and sexy it would take every member of the gang I used to run with to tear me away from her now.

"You can't hum."

"What?" she asks, her head going back.

"When you hum, it distracts me. When I'm distracted, I can't focus. A guy needs his focus when using power tools, otherwise it could be disastrous."

"Oh," she says. "I'm sorry." She flashes long lashes at me. "What can the girl do to help the boy get focused again?"

I grin as she steps into our game, one I know better than to play again. But I guess on some level referring to each other as the boy and girl helps keep a measure of distance— keep the sex impersonal.

"The boy probably needs the girl naked again." I touch her throat, run my hand down the long length of it. I cup her rib cage, brush my thumbs over her nipples, and revel as they harden beneath my ministrations. "He probably needs these in his mouth again, too. Greedy boy that he is."

She shrugs casually, but heat is crawling into her cheeks, a hot flush that rattles what little control I have. "If that's what the boy needs, then that's what the boy needs."

"It's not all he needs."

"No?"

"He needs the girl straddling him, so he can put his cock all the way up inside her again."

She goes still, and breathes for a few seconds, like words are momentarily lost on her. "If the girl wants her deck done and is the one responsible for the distraction in the first place, then she must do what the boy needs to get him focused again, don't you think?"

I cock my head, my gaze moving over her face. She asked for one night, but the needy look on her face speaks volumes and fucks with my ability to think with clarity. Still, there is a part of me that needs to hear her say it. "The girl wants?"

"The girl wants," she whispers, her hands going to the buckle on my tool belt. As she releases it, I sink into her warm, wet mouth, and taste mint on her tongue. Heaven. Pure fucking heaven. Hot and hungry, I practically attack her mouth with mine. Christ, if I'm not careful I could lose myself in her sweetness. But I'm no longer that dreamer from days long gone, and lessons learned taught me to always exercise caution—especially with women like her.

I reach down and slide a hand between her legs. I love these little dresses she wears, they give me such quick access to the spot my body craves. A little feathery breath escapes her mouth as I slide my hand upward, but this time I go still, and my cock rages against my zipper when I find her bare, completely naked beneath her dress.

"You're not wearing any panties," I growl.

She looks down shyly—innocently—but I don't miss the

mischievousness in her eyes. The damn girl knew what she was doing all along. She can feign innocence all she wants, but dammit, she'd been luring me to her with those soft, sexy hums.

"Panties are overrated," she whispers.

"Fucking right they are." I back up and pull her with me. My knees hit the sofa and I sit, dragging her onto my lap so she can straddle me. Her sex lips widen and hug my cock through my pants. I piston up and rub her clit with the rough flap over my zipper.

"Jamie," she murmurs, and grinds against me, creating friction and heat for the both of us. Her body is so needy for me again, mine so needy for hers, if I knew what was good for me, I'd run a hundred fucking miles in the other direction. But when was the last time I'd ever done what was good for me? I guess I'll just add this to my latest list of bad decisions.

"The girl missed my cock?"

"Yes."

My pulse thrums at her openness. "The girl has been aching to have it in here again," I whisper as I rub her clit. She lifts, giving me space to touch her. I slip a finger into her pussy, and it's insane how wet she is. "I believe you've been thinking about the boy all day, and all the dirty things you want him to do to you."

"Does the boy have any idea how hot he is with his tool belt on?"

I grin. "So it's the tool belt you want?"

She reaches between our bodies to unhook my pants. My nerve endings fire at the hiss of the zipper, the anticipation of what's to come. When my cock springs free, she closes her hands over it. "No. She wants what's underneath it."

She strokes me, and I finger fuck her as her warm hands race the length of me. "I'm going to make you come so hard for me again, Kylee," I whisper, and her eyes roll back as her head sways from side to side. I push another finger into her and she whimpers. "I'm going to have all of you before we're done," I say. "I'm going to fuck every inch of you."

She gasps, but it's followed by a moan when I brush her clit with my thumb. I tease the hot bud, change the rhythm and pressure until her hands still on my cock, her only thoughts on what I'm doing between her legs.

"Ride my fingers. Fuck them for me." I hold my fingers still and she lifts herself up and falls down. "That's it. Show me what a dirty girl you are." She cries out at my filthy words and comes down hard on my fingers. Clearly she likes it when I talk this way. I wiggle my fingers inside her, penetrate her deeply. "You don't need my cock at all. Look at you, getting all hot and wet and ready to come from my fingers."

She moans, and my cock leaks. Seeing her come undone like this is the sexiest fucking thing, and I'm seconds from shooting off a load. But I don't want to, not yet. I touch her mouth, shove my finger inside. Her lips close around me. "Does the girl want my cock in here?"

Instead of answering, she sucks my finger in, and I sink into the sofa, my cock so goddamn hard, I'm sure I'm going to rupture. She lifts, slams back down, and lifts again. Man, when my cock is in her, she's going to take me deeper than ever before. Her breathing is erratic, her cheeks a deeper shade of pink. Fuck, she's there already and we'd only just gotten started.

"The girl wants it all," she cries out, and shatters around my finger, comes completely undone, like a boneless rag doll. Her cum is so hot it scorches my flesh and it drips down my fingers. Fuck, if I don't get my cock inside her this very second I'm going to die. I'm sure of it. Sucking me off will have to wait, with my life being on the line and all. I grip her hips, and pull her hot cunt down onto my cock. Her heat sears me, sizzles through my body and detonates all my brain cells. I've never felt anything like it before, and I'm too far gone, too lost in sweet Kylee's heat, to consider why.

We fuck hard. I lift as she comes down, and we quickly create a rhythm. My body aches, my brain spinning like a hamster on a wheel. Her mouth parts, and her tongue slides across her lush lips leaving a smooth trail my cock wants to smudge. Fuck. I'll get my dick in there again, get it in every hole as we both finish scratching this itch, but right now, my cock is exactly where it's supposed to be. High inside her. I grip her shoulders and pull her down hard. She cries out, her sweet pussy devouring my cock until I'm balls fucking deep. I press my mouth to her breasts, kiss her nipples through her dress, and breathe in her scent.

Consumed, I fuck harder, hot and hungry and so goddamn needy it scares me a little bit. But I can't think about that right now. My cock is throbbing, aching to get off. Jesus, I haven't felt like this since I was a hormonal teen. Her lips close over mine, a steady deepening that smashes my last vestige of control. I squeeze my eyes shut and shoot my load high inside her. Her sweet cunt milks my shaft, massages every last drop of cum from my dick. Fucking amazing.

Her hands cup my face, and she's making a sexy mewling sound, as we lightly exchange kisses, both of us gasping for air as our lips eat at each other. But then suddenly my breath freezes in my lungs. Son of a fucking bitch. I didn't use a condom. I have never, ever been so lust-drunk that I'd forgotten a condom before. Christ, no wonder it felt so incredible. Then again would it have felt this amazing with someone who wasn't Kylee? I swallow against that worrisome thought and hope to hell she's on the pill. This thing between us is temporary and while she might want kids, they aren't in my future—at least not with her. I cup her head. I pull back and her eyes widen when they meet mine—see the horror.

"Jamie," she says, her voice wavering. "What?"

"I'm sorry, Kylee. I forgot to use a condom."

She swallows, and as her eyes widen with that revelation, my gut clenches. "I can't believe it." She blinks rapidly and her hair falls over her shoulders as she shakes her head. "I've never had sex without protection before." Her shoulders curl in and she hugs herself. "Not that I've been with many guys, but still."

"I've never had sex without a condom either, Kylee. I'm clean, but please, tell me you're on the pill, otherwise we need to go to the drugstore."

"I am," she says, and I exhale sharply, as I ride the wave of relief. "Kids aren't in my future," she adds.

"Good," I say, in regards to the pill, not her comment about not wanting kids. Even though the sadness behind her statement has piqued my curiosity, I don't ask for an explanation. I can't help but wonder, though, she's a girl who has it all, so why wouldn't kids be in her future? Since it's none of my business, and it's best not to get too close, I don't ask. Instead, I lift her from my cock and settle her on my lap.

She smiles at me, and her warm fingers, so soft against my skin, brush my hair from my face. "Is the boy able to focus now?"

Not even a little. Fuck, how can a guy expect to get any work done with a sexy little thing like Kylee a fuck away.

"The girl is going to have to get another hobby. One that doesn't involve humming."

And hopefully that hobby takes her away from the house during the day. She touches my cock, and it instantly thickens. Of course it does. It's a traitorous bastard.

"I believe she found one," she murmurs as she bends forward, taking me so deep into her throat, humming is impossible.

I am so fucked.

6

KYLEE

As I check the time and clean up my sewing room, I find myself humming again. My mind instantly rushes back to hours earlier, and I put my hand over my mouth to stifle the sound, but it's too late.

"Kylee," Jamie growls from the other side of the window, and I chuckle.

"Sorry." I step up to the window and look at the gorgeous man ripping apart my back deck. He's the epitome of virile male. Rock hard, fierce, a guy not to fuck with, yet I've been doing just that, and it's been damn amazing. "Can I get you a drink?" I ask as a peace offering. "I made some fresh lemonade."

"Yeah," he grumbles, and wipes his brow in such a guy way my ovaries clench. Seriously, I'm not making that shit up. My ovaries are actually clenching at the sexy sight of him. How could they not, right? I stare at him, memorize his hard body, take in the long, hard length of him so I can draw on it later when I'm back in Atlanta, stuck in a job I don't want. I commit broad shoulders that taper to a trim waist and washboard abs to memory. Everything about this man exudes power, strength, an animal unleashed, and most times I can barely catch my breath when I'm around him. I've never seen a body with so many tattoos, never thought I would like it or find it sexy, but on Jamie it just works. Everything works, even his too-long hair, which keeps falling into his eyes.

Drenched between my legs—again—I leave the sewing room and hurry to the kitchen, but my phone rings. I fish it from my purse and when I see my dad's number, reality hits me over the head like one of the cold Atlantic waves from my backyard view.

I stand there, debating whether to answer or not, but if I don't, he'll probably fly out here and check up on me. I slide my finger across the screen and lower my voice.

"Hi Dad," I say quietly.

"Kylee," he says. "How are things at the cottage? I'm sure everything is to your liking."

"It's beautiful here," I say, not a lie. I try to cover the phone, to hush the sound of the saw in the background.

"Trevor said you'd love it there. He said he's hoping to find some time to visit himself this summer."

Trevor, God. I so do not want to hear about the man my father is trying to set me up with. Yeah, he might have summered here his whole life, told Dad I'd love the place, which is what prompted him to buy this house in the first place, but that does not mean I want to spend time with him here. Seeing him in Atlanta is enough for me.

Outside I watch Jamie's muscles flex and relax again, and because he keeps distracting me, I turn my back to him and try to focus on my father and our conversation.

"What's all that noise?" he asks.

My entire body stiffens. The man is a million miles away, yet he still has the ability to put me on the defense. "Oh, the back deck was rotten, so I thought I should replace it."

He goes quiet, and I can practically see him now, rubbing his chin and nodding his head as he deliberates on whether or not replacing the rotting deck is a good investment.

"Well, if you think it was in need of replacing, I'm sure you're right. A new deck will only add to the value in the end."

And there you have it.

With my father, everything is about money and stature—everything Jamie is not—and Trevor, well, he's Dad's Mini-Me in every way. Maybe that's why I'm attracted to Jamie. They say opposites attract. As soon as Jamie passes through my thoughts, he appears in front of me.

"I have to go. Talk soon," I say quickly. I don't need Dad asking questions about my contractor or why he's inside my cottage. I'm about to set the phone down when it pings, indicating a text coming in. I give it a quick glance and stiffen when I see the text from Trevor, asking me how I like the place. Ignoring it, I shove the phone into my purse, out of sight. The phone keeps pinging, more texts, and I slide my hand into my purse to turn off the volume.

Jamie narrows his eyes, his gaze moving over my face, and I relax my shoulders to present calm. "Everything okay?" he asks.

"Fine," I say and hope my voice sounds as light as I'm trying to make it. Jamie and I are simply having sex, albeit great sex. He doesn't need to know what's going on in my life, just like I don't need to know what's going on in his. My problems aren't his, and his problems aren't mine. "Let me get you that drink." I race to the kitchen and pour the lemonade. I turn to take it to him outside, but find him leaning against the doorjamb, watching me carefully. "Here you go."

I hand him the drink and his throat works as he swallows the entire contents in a few gulps. "More?" I ask. He wipes the back of his mouth with his hand and shakes his head.

"I'm good. Are you?" He still has that strange, worried look on his face.

"I'm good. I was just cleaning up and getting ready for Gram and Summer."

His head rears back. "Gram and Summer?"

"We're going into Hope Falls today, remember?"

He narrows his eyes like he's checking his memory bank. "I remember them mentioning it. Didn't think it would be something you were interested in though."

"No? Why not?"

He opens his mouth, but a noise behind us has him closing it again. He spins, and both Gram and Summer storm into my place like they own it. Okay, maybe that's not true for Summer. With baby on board, she's much slower than her animated Gram.

Jamie jumps back, physically and emotionally. What the heck? I look at him but he avoids my gaze. Okay, obviously he doesn't want anyone to know what we've been up to behind closed doors. Maybe he doesn't want to give anyone the wrong idea that we're an item, or heck, maybe I embarrass him. Either way, it's a good reminder that what we're doing is temporary and between us only.

"I haven't been in here since the Reddens owned it," Gram says, glancing around at the furnishings.

I follow her gaze. "I haven't really had a chance to make it mine yet," I say. "It came furnished, and I'm only here until the end of the summer, so I wasn't sure about putting all the work into it. The deck though, that was a hazard."

"On that note, I'll get back to it." Jamie turns to go, but Gram stops him.

"Kiss your grandmother first." Gram taps her cheek and I grin as Jamie, all tough and rough, mellows into such a softie around her. For a man who has such a softness in him, he sure is an animal in the bedroom.

"Wait, Jamie," I say quickly and he goes still.

He turns again, and I grab the suntan lotion from the counter. "Your shoulders are burning." I toss it to him and he catches it.

Murderous eyes lock with mine for a long moment, a raging storm in a tropical forest, then he tears his gaze away and heads toward the screen door. "Thanks," he mumbles.

Summer breaks the uneasy tension before it expands and questions are asked by rubbing her stomach. "We'd better get going. Someone here is anxious for a Grande Americano."

I momentarily think about asking Jamie if he'd like me to bring him something back, but after that deadly glare, I think twice about it.

As I follow the women outside, leaving Jamie in charge of my cottage, I turn the corner and expect to see Gram's big truck. Instead I see one even bigger, with two-row seating and a long truck bed.

Summer pulls out her keys and I frown. "You okay to drive?" I ask, and point to my car. "We could take mine."

"I'm fine. Besides, we need the truck to fit the crib."

Oh right, I'd forgotten the purpose of our trip. "When are you due?"

"Not for three more weeks, but with the way I feel, I'm beginning to wonder if they mixed up the dates."

"How are you feeling?" I ask.

"Let's put it this way, I'm afraid to go too close to the water when I walk Scout. I don't want anyone to mistake me for a washed-up beluga. Next baby is going to be a winter baby. When you have kids, keep the heat in mind."

I laugh. "Poor you, but no kids are in my future." I make a move to jump into the bench seat in the back when Gram stops me. "Nope, you ride up front."

I open my mouth to protest, but when she scowls at me, I meet Summer's eyes and she grins. It's the same grin that

Benny gave me, one that says don't mess with Gram. "Besides," Gram adds. "I've driven with Summer before, and I'm much safer back here."

"Hey," Summer warns, but she's laughing hard. "I'm a good driver. That old truck was just too big for me."

"And this one isn't?" Gram retaliates.

I slide into the passenger seat and sense a story, but I guess Summer will tell me when she's ready. I glace at Summer's protruding stomach as she tries to get behind the steering wheel. Honestly, I can't believe that in all the children and grandkids, there has never been a girl. I can see how much Gram treats Summer likes she's one of her own. The two clearly have a special bond. I buckle up, just in case, as Summer backs out of the driveway.

As we pass her place she points. "That's where Sean and I live."

"I wasn't sure which one was yours." I glance at the chiropractor sign and turn to her. "You're a chiropractor?"

She nods, and a smile pulls at her mouth. She goes quiet for a moment, like she's remembering something. "I moved here from SoCal last year."

"You're a long way from home," I say.

"Nope. This is home. This is where I've always belonged." She meets Gram's eyes in the rearview mirror and my stomach clenches. These women are so close it makes me long for the same. The only time I ever heard from my grandparents was around the holidays when they sent a card with an impersonal check. I didn't want their money. I wanted their love, their friendship. But there is no sense in thinking about that now. I just want to enjoy the company of these ladies for today.

We chat about Summer's upcoming baby shower at the local bar, Winchesters, where she used to work before opening her chiropractic business. It seems odd to me that she worked as a bartender when she was a certified chiropractor, but I don't say anything. I'm delighted when they invite me to the shower this weekend and secretly grin at my surprise, pleased with the original outfits I designed. Jamie said she'd like them and I'm hoping he's right. Okay, stop thinking about Jamie already.

We get to Starbucks and we all place our orders, then slowly drive down the main street to the furniture outlet where she bought her crib. All the guys seem so handy, I'm surprised one of them hadn't made one themselves.

I sip my latte as Gram goes to the back of the truck. She opens the cover and I see containers full of food.

"What's all this?" I ask.

"Last night's leftovers."

I look at her confused. "What are you doing with them?"

"You see that building over there?" I turn and take in a brick building on the corner. "That's Hope Falls' shelter. For women and children who've fled domestic violence. I always make a little extra for Sunday dinner, so I can share."

My heart squeezes, and I reach into the truck to help with the containers. I want to say something. I try to say something. But there is a lump in my throat, so I just close my mouth and follow Gram to the shelter while Summer goes in search of a public bathroom. According to her, she knows every public bathroom in all the towns hugging Blue Bay. That certainly doesn't make me want to hurry and get pregnant.

I have no idea what to expect when we enter the shelter. The truth is, I've never seen one. I was raised in a privileged area of town, and I might lament that my father is all about power and prestige—and does pro bono work because it looks good to the public. Lord knows he'd never do it for selfless reasons—but how am I any better? I grew up wanting for nothing, yet I don't see myself running out to help those less fortunate than I am. Since actions speak louder than words, what am I going to do to change that? Gram here might not come from the same kind of wealth I have, but she gives what little she has, and that makes her a much better person than me.

A woman greets us and I stand back as she and Gram chat, then Gram passes her the containers. "Come along, Kylee," Gram says to me and we walk down a long hall until we reach what looks like a child's play area. A young girl, I'm guessing she's around four, comes running when she seems Gram. Gram bends and the little girl gives her a kiss on the cheek. Gram beams, and I smile. I really hope Summer is having a girl, although I'm sure Gram would be fine with a boy, too. I've seen her grandsons. She did a great job with them.

"Katrina, have you been a good girl this week?" Gram asks and taps her on her pert little nose.

"I'm always a good girl," she says, a slight lisp with her letter S.

"Then I have something special for you."

"Cupcake!" Katrina squeals.

The little girl claps her hands and her mother, a thin woman with dark circles under her eyes, comes out to join us. She goes down on one knee and puts her arm around Katrina. The bond between this mother and daughter is a powerful one, and my heart squeezes again, reinforcing my decision not to have children. A mother can't bond with her child if she's never there.

"You're going to spoil her," the mother says.

Gram laughs. "She deserves to be spoiled."

"Why don't you run into the kitchen and see about that cupcake," Gram says.

The little girl nods and says, "I made something for you." Katrina disappears into the kitchen, leaving the adults to talk.

The conversation turns serious. "How are you, Miranda?"

"We're doing good," Miranda says, but I can tell her smile is forced. She's clearly trying to make the best out of a bad situation, and my heart goes out to her.

"Work?"

"Not yet, but I'm still looking."

"Oh, my goodness, beg my pardon." Gram says, putting her arm around my waist and pulling me closer to her. "Miranda, this is Kylee. Kylee, this is Miranda. Kylee just bought one of the cottages in Blue Bay. Jamie is replacing her deck and she's helping Summer and me pick up the crib for the baby."

We exchange a handshake and Katrina comes running back with a picture in one hand, a sweet treat in the other, and a ring of chocolate around her mouth. She hands the picture to Gram. It's a little girl riding a horse. "Why Katrina, this is gorgeous. I'll put it next to the last one." My mind instantly goes back to Sunday dinner. Gram had drawings on her fridge but I didn't stop to give them a second thought. "You're going to be a famous artist someday, like Kylee here."

The little girl's eyes go wide. "You're an artist?"

"Well, I design clothes," I say. I look her over, and can't help but think that one or two of the dresses I have sitting in a tote would look so cute on her.

Just then Summer comes in and she greets Miranda and Katrina. After a few more exchanges Gram sends us to get the crib, telling us she has a few more people she'd like to talk to.

We head out into the sunshine, and I feel a little odd deep in my gut. This is a side of life I've heard about, of course, but have never really seen.

"That's a nice thing Gram does." She is a very selfless woman, and I could only aspire to be like her.

Summer nods. "She's one of a kind, isn't she?"

"I really like her." I think about the goodwill at Dad's company. Don't get me wrong, it's great, but it's just so . . . I rack my brain but can't come up with the right word to describe it. Regardless, what Gram does, this one-on-one connection, is so meaningful. She really cares about the families, and they obviously care about her too.

"I'm hungry," Summer says, and rubs her stomach. "Why don't we find a café and grab a bite after we get the crib loaded?"

"I could eat," I say, my stomach taking that moment to grumble. I had quite the workout earlier that morning and was in such a hurry to get ready that I forgot to eat.

"Great, let's get the crib, then I'll text Gram to meet us."

"Gram texts?" I say, my mouth agape.

Summer laughs. "Gram does a lot of things."

At the mention of texting, my phone pings. Could it be Gram? Nah, she doesn't have my number. At least I don't think she has it. I reach into my purse and when I see it's yet another text from Trevor, I frown. If I don't answer him, he'll never let up, but answering him just might lead him to believe I want his texts—that there is more between us. I quickly type back, *things are good,* and nothing more, then drop my phone back into my purse, hoping that will put an end to his texts.

Summer glances at me as we make our way into the department store. "Everything okay?"

Fine," I say injecting a lightness into my tone as Summer hands her slip to the guy at the pick-up counter. When she catches me grinning she asks, "What?"

"I don't know. This is just so small-town. Back home we'd

just order from Amazon and it would be delivered in a day or two."

"I know. It was like that in SoCal too. Today everything is about instant gratification, and it's so impersonal, right?"

Impersonal, that's it. That's the word I was searching for. The donations my dad's company makes are so impersonal, much like the way I've run my life, really. Sadly.

The delivery guy wheels out a big box with a picture of a pretty white crib on it.

"It's gorgeous," I say.

"Not as beautiful as the one Jared made."

"Really? If Jared made one, why do you need this one?"

"It's an extra crib for Gram's place. For when she babysits, plus I'm going to be staying with her for a bit after the baby is born."

"Oh, I didn't realize."

There is a deep sadness on her face when she says, "I was an only child and my mom died young. I don't really have a lot of experience and need Gram to show me a few things. She offered to stay with us at the cottage, but I'd rather not put her out like that. She loves retiring to her own bedroom at night, and no kitchen can compete with hers," she adds with a grin. "So Sean and I are going to stay there for a few days instead. And really, I think it will be nice to be surrounded by the whole family those first few days."

"That's so nice."

"What about you? Do you have family?"

"My dad is a lawyer in Atlanta. Mom was a lawyer too, but she died a few years back, and I didn't have any siblings."

"I'm sorry about your mom. I bet she would have been proud that you followed in their footsteps."

I force a smile. "For sure. So how long will you be staying with Gram?" I ask.

"For at least a week. I'm hoping Jamie will stay at the beach and take care of Scout."

Jamie at the cottage, a few doors down. Talk about temptation.

She crinkles her nose. "Maybe you could check in on him once in a while. Make sure he remembers to feed and walk Scout. Sometimes that boy is such a dreamer, I think if Gram didn't feed all the grandsons once in a while he'd starve."

"Sure," I say. I could also make sure he's fed, well rested . . . and well fucked.

"He always was a dreamer, you know. Ever since we were kids."

She knew the guys when she was young? Shocked by this, I'm about to press when Summer goes stiff. For a second I think she's having labor pains, but then I follow her gaze. Up ahead I see a guy coming our way. He's very well put-together in khaki pants and a polo shirt, and looks more like he's a guy I'd associate with, and not one Summer or the Owens boys would know. His blue eyes flash over Summer, like he's trying to place her, then slide to mine. As he takes me in, a strange feeling of familiarity moves through me. Do I know this guy?

My gaze goes from the guy, to Summer, back to the guy again and I rack my brain as he breezes past, but when I see the alarm on Summer's face my steps slow. "What's wrong?" I ask quickly.

"Nothing . . . just that's Ben Jackinoff." She gives me a nudge to keep me in motion.

"Ben Jackinoff?" I say. "What kind of name is that?"

"It's what the guys used to call him when we were young."

"So he's from around here?"

"No, not really."

I'm not sure who the guy is, but he sure has Summer flustered, and it seems to me after hanging out with the Owens crew, agitating Summer takes a great deal. "I take it they didn't like him too much."

Then, as if she'd said too much, she hooks her arm in mine and points to Gram coming from the shelter. But if they guys hated him, I want to know more.

"Who is he?" I press.

Her eyes widen, and she touches my shoulder in warning. "The father of some horrible guys, and no one you want to know, okay?"

What the hell is going on?

7

JAMIE

"Why the hell do I have to be here?"

Sean kicks me from beneath the table. "What the fuck's the matter with you?"

I glare at my brother as the army known as the Owens boys occupies the back table at Winchesters, which is currently closed to the public for Summer's private baby shower—which I was forcefully dragged to.

I tip my beer, take a long pull, and drop it onto the scarred table harder than necessary. "Do you even have to ask?"

"Come on bro, it's not so bad," Jared says, as his predatory gaze roams the room. "Look at all the pussy." When his eyes move over Kylee, I fist my hand, but the movement doesn't go unnoticed by Sean or Ryan. Man, I could only imagine what they'd say if they knew I was messing around in her backyard. Yeah, Sean put me on her job, but the other guys were tied up, and when it came right down to it, I was the right guy for the job, no matter what I told Kylee. Sean didn't do it to hook us up or torture me. At least I don't think. Then again . . . Nah, he'd never do that to me. He knows my motto as well as the rest of them.

"Leave it to Jared to turn a baby shower into his personal fucking whorehouse," Tyler says as he cracks his knuckles. Jared jumps up, ready to spar with Tyler, but Sean's glare has them both sitting down again.

"Summer wanted us all here, so we're all here. So quit your fucking sulking," he says, and we all sink back into our chairs.

From behind the counter, Adam cracks another eight beers and hands them to Stacy the bartender, who has been giving Jacob the evil eye all night. That's what he gets for up and leaving her the night of their prom. If I were him, I'd think twice before drinking from any open bottle she handed me.

Oohs and *ahhs* come from the women seated around a row of tables pushed together. Pretty much half the town came out for the shower. Even Officer Walker is here—a guy we all have a history with. But I'm not surprised to see the room so crowded. Everyone fell in love with Summer the second she returned to Blue Bay, even though she was going under the alias of Jenna Garridy. But that's a story for another time. Still, she spent a lot of time here as a kid, a lot of time with Sean, and as far as I'm concerned, she's as much a part of Blue Bay as I am.

I look around the room, trying to focus on anything and anyone other than Kylee. But my attempt is futile. My gaze keeps straying back to her. I'm actually surprised to see her here. In less than a week, she was taken in by my family, bonded with Gram and Summer, and seems to have made quite a few friends with the locals herself. Surprising really, because most times the locals and summer vacationers don't mix on a social level. My ex mingled with the locals too, and look how that turned out. Like Kylee, she was also sweet and kind. Before she, you know, ruined my life and all.

Last I heard two of her brothers had become SEALs, although one was injured in the line of duty and I lost track of him. The other two became lawyers like their father. That's the kind of shit that runs in a rich family. I scoff. In not-so-rich ones too, considering all eight of us guys are back to get Dad's business back in the black and doing a damn fine job of it too.

I push from my chair and head toward the hall leading to the bathroom when Officer Walker stops me. I stiffen, always my first reaction around the police. "Walker," I say.

"Jamie," he says and narrows his eyes, like he can see into my soul and knows all the dirty things I've been doing with a summer vacationer who is totally off-limits to me. "Things good?"

"Yeah."

"I hear you're doing some work on the Jensen cottage."

"New deck," I say, and he widens his stance, meets my gaze directly.

"No troubles?" he asks, the atmosphere heavy with things unsaid, things he doesn't need to say for me to get the warning he's throwing my way. He was the officer who arrested me all those years ago, and he's warning me to keep my hands to myself and my dick in my pants.

Too fucking late for that.

"No troubles," I say.

He nods. "Glad to hear it."

I maintain eye contact and get the strange sense that there is more going on here, that he knows something I don't, and I don't fucking like it. I'm about to ask when Summer shrieks, and I turn to see her open the last present, the two outfits from Kylee. But a strange, worried look comes over Kylee's face and she grabs her purse and darts down the long hallway, sliding past Walker and me. What the fuck?

"Later," I say to Walker and follow her, but she disappears

into the girl's washroom. I'm about to keep going past it to the little boys' room when I hear her voice. Since it's a one-sided conversation, I'm guessing she's on her phone. Seems like she's trying to placate someone for not checking in earlier. Who the hell is she talking to? Her overprotective father? Jesus, that thought should have me running out the fucking door and back to New Orleans. But then her voice goes lower, and it raises alarm bells inside me. I listen closer, even though it's none of my business. I only followed her because she seemed upset about something.

I push off the wall and turn, but when I do, she comes out and walks right in to me. She stumbles a bit, and I slide my hand around her back. The touch sends heat through me, and her look of concerns morphs into desire, a pink flush on her cheek.

Goddamn that pink flush. That and her humming are what got me into trouble earlier in the week when I practically attacked her in the sewing room. Since then I've been trying my hardest to keep my distance from her, but Jesus, now that I have her in my arms again, I'm pretty certain I'm not going to walk out of this place without fucking her again.

"Everything okay?" I ask.

"Yeah, ah, I was just chatting with my father."

Ah, so it was the protective father.

"He was just checking in with me to see if I was good," she adds.

"Are you good, Kylee?"

I dip my head, and when she wets her mouth, I brush my thumb over her bottom lip. She glances up and down the hall, like she's afraid someone might stumble upon us. Truthfully, I don't want to get caught either. Summer and Gram might have bonded with her, but I'm sure any one of my brothers or cousins would cut off my nuts if they knew I'd fucked her more than once and wanted to continue to fuck her for the remainder of the summer. Which I can't do.

Then again, if I know what I'm getting into and we both know the score, why shouldn't we? A sound catches in my throat. I'm not a stupid dreamer anymore, about to plan a future with a girl who's only out for a good time. If I'm only out for a good time, then why can't we have a secret affair?

"I'm . . . good," she says.

"You sure about that?"

I back her up, open the door to the women's bathroom, and usher her in. "Jamie," She whispers breathlessly. "What are you doing?"

"I need to fuck you," I admit. "Every night this week, I took my cock into my hands, wishing it was inside you . . . wishing it was in here." I push my thumb into her mouth, and her eyes go wider. I search her face. "Does the girl need that?" I take my finger from her mouth and brush her hair from her face. Jesus, she's so pretty.

"Here?"

I shake my head, remembering who I'm with. Girls like Kylee don't fuck in bathrooms. "If you—"

"I do," she says, surprising me. "I just . . . what if someone catches us?"

Her words give me pause. *She doesn't want to get caught slumming with me.* Old lessons come racing back. Fuck, man, I shouldn't be doing this. No matter how much my body craves hers, I need to put a stop to this here and now.

"I—" I begin, but she cuts me off.

"I know you don't want anyone to know about us."

Shit.

Fuck.

"Kylee, it's just . . ." Shit, what am I supposed to say? I'm going against my own motto, and not only will my brothers kick my ass for it, nothing good can come from it. But before

I say anything, a loud noise in the dining room draws my attention.

I back away from Kylee and work to marshal my dick. "What the hell?"

"We'd better go check," Kylee says, and I follow her out of the bathroom. We round the corner and see Sean with his arms around Summer, leading her to the front door while the others all pack up the gifts and put the room back together.

"What's going on?" I ask.

"Summer's water broke. We're about to be uncles, bro," Jared says, patting me on the back as his gaze goes from me to Kylee. I step away from her and help pack things up.

"Gram!" Summer calls out. "Drive with us."

Gram grabs her purse and a few of my brothers follow them out, and I catch Sean pushing them away as they fuss about Summer. I shake my head. That kid is going to be spoiled. As I think about that my heart grows a bit heavy. Mom and Dad would have loved having a grandchild.

"Are you going to the hospital?" Kylee asks me quietly, pulling me from my thoughts. I nod, and she pushes my hand away as I gather up bags. "Then go. I've got this." Kylee looks at the crowd. "Go be with your family. I'll take all these things back to the house."

I reach into my pocket and give Sean's house key to Kylee. "I'm in charge of Scout while Summer is in the hospital. Why don't you bring all this stuff there, and if you wouldn't mind taking Scout for a quick walk, I'd appreciate it. I can get the key from you later."

She nods. "Okay."

I'm about to leave when her knuckles brush mine, and there is a small—okay, huge—part of me that wishes she were going to the hospital with me. But she's not family and never will be.

"Thanks," I say.

I follow everyone out and cast a quick glance behind me in time to see Stacy give Kylee a hand with the bags. I hop on my bike and make my way to the hospital, which is only about a ten-minute drive in the direction of Hope Falls. I find my brothers and cousins pacing inside the waiting room and I flop down onto one of the chairs. It's going to be a long-ass night, that's for sure. As we all sit around we talk about the usual business while a few of the guys check out the nurses. We've been here all of ten minutes and I think Tyler already has a date.

I push from my chair, antsy. I never did like hospitals, especially after having spent weeks in one after I was nearly beaten to death. I make my way to the vending machine and try not to think about the beating that landed me here. I've only been back a year and haven't run into my ex's asshole brothers. They haven't sold their cottage, but if they know what's good for them, they'd better not show their faces around here now that I'm back.

I grab a coffee, take a sip, and wince. Jesus Christ, this has to be the worst coffee. I hand it to Ryan. That guy will drink anything. Minutes turn into hours, and we're all restless, watching some rerun of *Friends* on TV. Gram just gave us an update that Summer is doing well, and she's begun dilating. Yeah, 'cause I needed to know that.

I jump up, ready to try the vending machine coffee again, when Kylee comes in carrying two trays with Starbucks coffee. The guys all jump up and help themselves.

"I have another tray in the car," she says to me.

"You didn't have to do this," I say, and with my back to the guys, blocking her from their view, I tug at one of the lower buttons on her sundress, bringing her a little closer to me. Her eyes briefly shut and a small mewling sound catches in her throat. My cock hardens. Fuck, I want her again.

"I wanted to," she says quietly. "It wasn't that far out of the way, and I figured you guys were in for a long night."

"Thank you."

"Want to help me with the last tray?" I follow her outside, and the cooler night air falls over me. "How is Summer?" she asks.

"She's begun dilating," I say, repeating what Gram told me, and steal a glance at her. When she sees the look on my face she starts laughing.

"I'm guessing you could have gone your whole life without ever having known that."

We reach her car and I turn her to press her back to the door. Her breathing changes as I gaze at her lips. "Yeah, but I can't go one more minute without this."

My mouth closes over hers and her soft purring sounds fill the silence of the night. I kiss her, devour her, slide my tongue into her mouth to taste the depths of her, wishing like hell we could finish what we started at Winchesters. I push against her body, and she moves, massaging my hard dick with her softness. Ravenous, I grip her hair, twist it around my palm and groan into her mouth. Her hands slide around me and I shift to touch her body, run my fingers along her curves.

I steadily deepen the kiss as we touch, our hands moving urgently, like we can't get close enough. We stay like that for a long time until headlights signal an approaching vehicle. I back off quickly when the sports car comes closer, when all I want is to stay right where I am and lose myself in her sweetness. As I catch the driver looking at us, a wave of unease moves through me. I have no idea why. I can't make out the guy's features, and he's obviously a vacationer with an expensive sports car like that, but something I can't quite identify niggles in the back of my brain.

"What was that for?" she asks.

"The coffee."

"I guess I should bring coffee more often, then," she says her voice breathless, as she adjusts her sundress.

I laugh and focus back in on her. "Just think what I would have done if you'd brought donuts, too."

A mischievous grin moves over her face. She reaches into the car, comes out with another tray of coffee and a box of donuts. She hands them to me and says, "I can't wait to find out."

8

KYLEE

I pace inside Summer and Sean's beautiful home, going from room to room and pausing outside the nursery. My heart squeezes as I take in the intricately designed crib Jared made, one that will undoubtedly be handed down from generation to generation. It's absolutely gorgeous and sends ribbons of longing through me.

Scout follows me around and when we reach the main room, she begins to whine. I've never had a dog before, even though I've always wanted one, and don't know the first thing about taking care of one. I've filled her water bowl and fed her. What else could she need? She jumps around me and trots to the door. Ah, that's it. She needs to go outside to do her business.

I open the front door, and she darts past me. "Scout," I yell, but the thick fog rolling in off the ocean obscures my vision. Great, just great. Jamie counted on me to take care of Scout, and the first night on the job, I've gone and lost her. I tug on my flats and zip up my sweater, the night air cold this time of the year.

I grab Scout's leash from the hook and hurry outside.

"Where are you?" I ask. I see her outline on the grass and walk toward her. She finishes doing her business and comes running at me. "My God, you have a lot of energy." She sees the leash in my hand and barks. "Want to go for a walk?"

She barks again, and I bend down and hook the leash to her collar. It's dark and foggy as we head toward the beach. I probably wouldn't walk it alone at night, especially if I were back in Atlanta, but feel a measure of comfort here in Blue Bay, where everyone knows everyone, and I can't forget that I have Scout by my side. She's big and has a ferocious bark that would scare away anyone who didn't know her. She prances beside me, and I smile down at her. We reach the water and she nips at the rolling waves. I breathe in the salty brine as the cold water races over my flats.

I'm far, far away from the hustle and bustle of Atlanta, that's for sure. But that thought dampens my mood. Soon enough I'll have to go back to reality and face a future that holds little appeal. But I don't want to think about that right now. I just want to live in the moment and enjoy the next few months. Scout starts barking and it pulls my thoughts back.

A shiver of unease works its way through my veins as she looks off in the distance and growls. I swallow against the tightness in my throat. She obviously sees or hears something I don't. Alrighty then. Totally creeped out and not at all interested to see what, or who, might emerge from the shadows, I tug Scout's leash and practically run all the way back to Summer's home. I hurry inside, grab my purse and Scout's big doggy bed, then rush back outside. Until Jamie returns, I'll feel much more comfortable at my place with the alarm on. I don't even know the code to Summer's. I lock the door and pant heavily as I run a few doors down. Okay, that's it. I need to get on the treadmill more often. Then again, my breathlessness could have more to do with the strange feeling I'm being watched.

I hurry inside, set the alarm, and pull the blinds. I probably shouldn't be as frightened as I am. If there were anyone on the beach, they probably wouldn't fuck with Jamie's woman. Well, technically I'm not his woman, and no one really knows what we're doing behind closed doors. Jamie obviously wants to keep our relationship a secret—judging by the way he backed away from me and acted distant when Gram and Summer came to pick me up for crib shopping, not to mention the way he immediately put distance between us when the car passed outside the hospital—and I'm okay with that. It's just a summer fling and it's none of anyone's business.

I unhook Scout and set her bed out for her. But first, she must explore every inch of my cottage and sniff every piece of furniture. "Come lay down, girl," I say and pat her big pillow. She walks to her bed, circles it a few times, then flops down to go to sleep. Damn I wish I could fall asleep that fast.

My cell phone rings, and I nearly jump out of my shoes. I hurry to my purse and grab it. When I see Jamie's number I relax a bit, the coiled tension in my body evaporating.

"Hey," I say, far too happy to hear from him.

"Hey yourself," he returns, his deep voice falling over me, a velvet caress against my flesh. A moment of silence and then, "You okay?"

"Yeah, why?" Jeez, I can't get anything him.

"You sound . . . off."

For a second I think about telling him I was creeped out down by the water, but then decide against it. He's not my protector, and really, this thing between us is just sex, right? "I was just out walking Scout and brought her back to my place. I set the alarm, but you know the code, right?"

"Yeah, why did you set the alarm? Most people don't even lock the doors in Blue Bay."

"Habit," I fib. Back in Atlanta, I always locked and

double-checked the doors. "How is Summer?" I ask, redirecting his focus. It's pretty amazing that she has so much support. Every brother and cousin is camped out at the hospital awaiting news. She's a lucky girl to have so many people love her.

"Still waiting. I think it's going to be a long night."

"Should I keep Scout here with me or bring her back to her place?"

"You should tell me what you're wearing."

I laugh, but his words do reinforce that our relationship is physical only. Good, cause that's what I want too. "You can't be serious?"

"Yeah, why not?" The heat behind his words goes right though me, and my body quakes, aching to see him naked again, run my hands over his hard body as he enters me. I remember the way his hard muscles bunched under my touch, the way his cock tightened in my mouth. I swallow against the dryness in my throat and search for my voice.

"Because you're at the hospital," I counter.

"All the more reason to tell me," he whispers, his voice so deep and hungry, it torments the needy spot between my legs. "Where are you right now?"

I walk to the sofa and sit. "I'm sitting on the sofa."

"Lie down for me."

I shake my head, as a little thrill moves through me. I've never had phone sex before, but hey, I've come this far with Jamie and have been having a lot of fun, so why not see where this takes us?

Straight down the road called trouble.

Ignoring that thought, I stretch out on the sofa. "Okay."

"You lying down?"

"Uh-huh."

"What are you wearing?"

"I'm in my sundress. The one I was wearing at the party."

"You look hot in that. You look hot in all those sexy dresses you make."

I chuckle, a nervous little sound that catches in my throat, but there is a part of me that is touched by the compliment. "Thank you," I say for lack of anything else. "What are you wearing?" I ask, even though I already know. The vision of Jamie in his low-slung jeans and snug T-shirt is something fantasies are made of.

"Same as earlier," he says. "But I wish I was naked with you right now. Are you wearing panties?"

"Yes."

"Where are your hands?"

I lift my head slightly to gaze over my body. "Well, one is on the phone and the other is resting on my stomach."

"Show me."

I shake my head even though he can't see me. "How am I supposed to do that?"

"Let's Skype."

"Jamie, you're at the hospital," I say, my voice full of reprimand, even though I find the idea perfectly delicious.

"I found a supply closet," he says, his voice soft. Positively intimate. "I'm in it alone, and all I can think about is fucking you again. Since I can't be there, I thought the best way to be close was like this."

This is all terribly inappropriate, but when it comes to Jamie, I just can't seem to help myself. I want to do all the dirty delightful things from the rough and tough guy who fucks like a god.

"You're crazy, you know that," I say and wrap my fingers tighter around my phone, lowering my voice to match his even though no one other than a snoring Scout is within earshot.

He gives a soft laugh, a dark, dangerous sound that triggers a needy reaction in me. Honest to God even though we're miles apart, a volatile sexual tension—enough to light up the string of houses on the beach during a blackout—still hangs heavy between us. This kind of electricity doesn't come along every day . . . or maybe never.

"That's one of the nicer things I've been called," he growls.

I roll my eyes. I don't believe that, of course. He's a dangerous guy with a sweet side, no matter what he says.

Careful Kylee . . .

"I'll text you my Skype name," he says, and I hear a rustling noise. What is he up to now? "Hang on."

I wait until the text comes in and then when his beautiful face materializes on my screen, his lusty green eyes a shade deeper, I shudder uncontrollably. My heart pounds faster, a fever burning through me.

"Can you put the phone somewhere so I can see all of you?"

I tug the coffee table closer and brace the phone up against the flowered centerpiece. Then I take my sweater off and toss it aside.

"How's this?"

"Good."

"I want to see all of you too," I say, trying not to sound as needy and desperate as I feel. He places the phone on something and backs up until I can see his body. God, he is so good-looking, it's utterly insane. Why hasn't some woman snatched him up by now?

"Pull your dress up."

I do as he says and pull it up to my waist. The air is cool against my flesh, but despite it my body grows hotter. I bite my lip, a tremble moving through me as I expose myself.

"Put your hands in your panties for me."

"Oh, God," I whisper, but since I'm too far gone into

playing out a fantasy to turn back now, I slowly slide my hand down my stomach and dip inside my lacy white panties.

He blows his hair off his face and I can almost feel it fall over my damp skin. "Stroke yourself for me."

I rub my clit, slide the pad of my finger over my swelling nub, and arch my back as delicious sensations rocket through me. I angle my head toward the phone when I hear the hiss of his zipper, and my heart speeds up. I can't believe he's going to get himself off in front of me, too. I watch, transfixed as he takes his gorgeous cock into his hands and strokes from base to crown. My throat tightens at the hot image. Seriously, though, that has to be the single most erotic thing I've ever seen. And to know he can't wait another second to be with me, that he had to find a supply closet, well, that just does something to me on a whole new level. I've never felt so wanted before. Never felt my stomach clench with this kind of need before either. It's scary how much I crave him. I've never needed another man's touch the way I need his, and the thing that really scares me is that when this is over, I fear this bad boy is going to ruin me for any other man—yet here I am, bending to his desires and giving him anything he asks for.

Just don't give your heart to a guy who doesn't want it.

"Jamie," I whisper and our eyes lock, the connection between us hitting like a damn sucker punch and driving all the air from my lungs. My God, this man . . .

He braces one hand on the wall, and continues to rub himself. "I need to see your breasts," he murmurs. I sit up and peel my dress over my head. I brush my thumbs over my nipples through the lace, just to tease him a bit, then unhook my bra.

"You are so fucking gorgeous," he says, his hand clutching his cock tighter and working the long length of it faster. It's seriously the hottest thing I've ever seen. "Wet your finger and rub those pretty pink nipples for me."

I put my finger into my mouth and suck on it for a bit. Jamie's tortured growl curls though me and triggers a deep craving inside me. A desperate sort of ache takes hold. I watch his hand stroke, see the hunger in his eyes. I slide my hands to my breasts and cup them. I swipe my wet finger over my hard nipple and close my eyes against the sensory overload.

"Tell me how they feel?"

"So good, Jamie," I murmur. "But missing you."

"My mouth is watering for a taste," he says. "Pinch them."

I pinch my nipples and my skin grows tight, little goose bumps breaking out on my flesh. Sensations blaze through me and I moan, the needy spot between my legs growing slicker. A low growl of longing sounds deep in his throat and pleasure forks through me.

"When I get back I'm going to slide my cock between your pretty tits, Kylee. I'm going to fuck your beautiful breasts and fill your mouth with my cum."

I gasp, his dirty teasing words sending heat straight to my sex.

"Sit up and face the phone," he commands softly. I swing my legs over the side of the sofa, the position affording him a better view of my naked body, and continue to stroke my nipples. Jamie grins at me.

"Fun, huh?"

"Yeah," I say. Even though we are having fun, oddly enough this feels far more intimate than anything we've done before—and we're not even in the same room. There's a new closeness between us, one that I can't explain, yet I can feel it in every fiber of my being—and that's not good. Not good at all.

Pushing those worrisome thoughts to the recess of my

brain, I say, "I just wish it was your hands on my body." His breathing changes, becomes heavier, and when it occurs to me how hot I'm making him I continue with, "My nipples ache for you, Jamie. They're so hard, all I can think about is you putting them in your mouth and sucking."

"Fuck," he grumbles, a new impatience thrumming through him. "Spread your legs, show me your pussy," his voice deepening to a growl.

I slowly spread my legs open, giving him an up-close view of my sex. "Touch yourself."

I slide my hand between my legs and stroke my clit, slowly circling my finger around it. As I stroke myself I stare at his hand and the hard way he's fisting his cock.

"Tell me about your pussy, Kylee. Are you wet?"

I rub my finger along my clit and then dip inside. I make a mewling sound and he grunts harder. I love watching his hand work his cock. Cum pools on the crown and I can almost taste the tang.

It's making me insanely wet. "I'm wet and hot for you."

"Close your eyes for a second. Pretend it's my tongue on you."

I do as he asks, and moan as my orgasm approaches. "I want that, Jamie. I want your tongue on me."

"You hurting for me, baby? You need my hard cock inside you?"

"I do," I manage to say as I push a finger inside my drenched sex, then brush it over my engorged clit.

"Wet your lips for me." I run my tongue over my lips and he says, "Wet them with your juices." He pulls on his cock and seeing him this aroused—for me—rattles me to my very core. "When I get back I want to taste you on your mouth." As pleasure sharpens and deepens between my legs, I pull my finger out from my sex and slide it over my mouth. "Fuck that's sexy. I'm going to put my cock in that sweet mouth of yours and fuck it. You're going to take me into your throat, Kylee, so fucking deep you're going to choke a bit. You want that? You want to choke on my cock?"

I whimper, and nod, my hair tangling beneath me, but I don't care. No, all I care about is the heat in my body and the filthy things this man is saying to me as he strokes his cock, hard.

"Good, now open your legs wider, and put your finger inside you."

I spread my legs as far as they will go, and push two fingers inside. My muscles swell around my probing fingers and my entire body breaks out in a hot flush. I close my eyes, pretend it's Jamie's cock, but I moan in distress, wanting the real thing.

"Fuck your fingers for me," he orders his voice rough.

I do as he asks, lift my hips as I slide my fingers into my sex and use my palm against my clit. For a long while he says nothing as we both moan and lose ourselves in our bodies like we're in a trance of sorts.

He finally breaks the quiet and asks, "Feel good?"

"Yes, but I need more," I respond, hungry for his hard cock, to be filled the way only he can fill me. "I need you."

"I'm going to fuck you so hard tonight, you're not going to be able to walk for a week," he says, the tendons on his neck so tight they look like they might snap. "I promise you that."

"Walking is overrated," I say and continue to plunge two fingers inside me. I rock my hips, pleasure intensifying between my legs.

He chuckles, but the sound is strained. "Keep touching yourself. I want us to come together."

I hiss as I work my fingers over my inflamed clit, a steady pulse of pleasure taunting me. I press down harder, rubbing with a maddening pace as I chase an orgasm.

"Fuck yeah," he says. "My dick is so hard for you. I can't wait to get inside you."

I can't believe we're actually doing this while he's in a supply closet at the hospital. It's dirty, naughty, and downright sexy. I love every second of it. I grind against my palm and his arm flexes as he strokes his cock.

"That's it. Rub yourself harder," he says and I swear to God I could come from his deep voice alone. "Work that sweet pussy for me." I squeeze my sex muscles, and the pleasure deepens. "Tell me how much you want my cock in you."

"Jamie," I cry out. "It's all I can think about."

"I'm going to fuck you everywhere, Kylee. Your mouth, your tits, even your sweet ass. I'm going to fucking ruin you, and you're going to let me."

His filthy words excite me. "Yes," I say, the thoughts of him taking me all those ways stealing my breath as I fixate on his hard cock. "I need that too."

He grunts. "I'm going to make you so hot, you're going to beg me to take you."

My mind spins, my body edgy, out of control, burning hotter than it ever has before. I whimper and writhe on the sofa, every muscle in my body tightening. "Jamie, I'm going to come."

"Me too." He grunts and it's followed by a loud moan.

"Show me," I say, completely exhilarated by what we're doing. My muscles clench hard, and I cry out as an orgasm rips through me. Jamie lifts his shirt and when he spurts cum all over his stomach, a second orgasm rolls through me.

Oh, my God, that is hot.

I sink back onto the sofa and struggle to breathe. Jamie's face comes into focus as he steps closer to his phone. His grin is dirty, mischievous, as he takes shallow breaths with me. We both go quiet for a long time, just looking at each other. I take in the sheen on his forehead, the dampness in his hair.

My gaze goes to his beautiful mouth, and he wets his bottom lip. My body ignites again. He looks away for a second, his body stilling.

"Shit, I have to sign off. Someone's coming."

Reality comes crashing back and I see him reach for something from the shelf. He quickly wipes himself clean, then does his pants back up. I shiver to think that any staff member could have walked in on him. How very risky of us, and so out of character for me. This man has flipped a switch on me, turning me from the good, obedient daughter to the naughty girlfriend willing to try anything once. Girlfriend? No, more like girl he's simply having a summer fling with.

As though reading my thoughts, he gives me a dirty, devilish grin that holds so much promise. "I'll see you soon, Kylee."

"Yeah, you will," I say, and lay boneless on the sofa, counting the minutes until he knocks on the door and fulfills all the promises he's made to me.

I shouldn't want him this badly. I know it. But God help me, I'm going to let that man ruin me in far too many ways.

9

JAMIE

It's two in the morning by the time I make it back to the beach. I open the door and reset the alarm. I take a few steps inside, and Scout's tail thumps on her bed when she hears me coming.

"Go back to sleep girl," I whisper, and tug off my T-shirt, exhausted and ready to climb into bed—with Kylee. Jesus fuck the thoughts of that shouldn't make me this goddamn happy. I'm about to head to the bedroom when I find the girl who's been plaguing my thoughts, even in sleep, crashed out on the sofa—likely waiting for me.

My heart misses a beat as I think about that, think about coming home to her after a hard day at work. I take her in, savor the moment, the quiet surrounding us as we lock the world out and us in.

Her hair is a tousled mess, and her body is curled up tight for warmth, an old throw blanket draped over her. She's never looked prettier. Her clothes are in a heap on the floor and my dick thickens when I see her phone still propped against the centerpiece on the coffee table. What we did was risky, inappropriate, but fuck, man, when it comes to her I can't seem to help myself. As much as I want to follow through with all the filthy things I swore I'd to do to her, with her—yeah, I want to take her hard and put my cock down her throat—she looks too sweet and too tired for me to wake her and ravage her the way I'd promised. I don't think that's what she needs from me right now, anyway, and it's not just a woman's prerogative to change her mind, right?

I gently pick her up and she stirs in my arms. "Shhh, go back to sleep," I whisper but her eyes go wide, startled, at the sound of my voice. Why the hell is she so spooked? "It's me," I say quickly to put her at ease, and her arms snake around my neck. "I've got you."

"Jamie," she says quietly, and I fucking love the sleepy sexy sound of my name on her tongue. "How is Summer?"

"She's resting now. She did great, and I am the proud uncle of a seven-pound baby boy named Devon Sean Owens."

"Another boy," she says and laughs softly, the sweet melodic sound seeping under my skin and stirring up my insides like a summer rainstorm over the ocean. "Poor Gram."

I laugh with her. "Gram is excited, but damn, she's going to be ragging on the rest of us to hurry up and give her a great-granddaughter." I readjust her in my arms and head for the hall. She goes quiet, almost too quiet as she rests her head against my bare chest, her breath hot on my skin. I stifle a yawn, but there is nothing I can do to ward off a shiver when she puts her finger on my chest and idly traces an old scar.

"Do you want kids, Jamie? Ever think about settling down?" she asks quietly, her mellow mood matching mine. I carry her down the hall to her bedroom and pull the sheets back on the bed. She shrugs from the sofa blanket wrapped around her slim shoulders as I set her down. My muscles bunch, and my cock tightens at her nakedness, her complete openness and lack of inhibition with me.

"I never really gave it much thought. I guess I don't really see myself as the father type, and as far as marriage is concerned, I'm not the kind of guy a girl brings home to Daddy." Her brow furrows like she's in deep thought and when she doesn't disagree—fuck knows I'm not the kind of guy she could ever take home, for more reasons than she knows—I drop to my knees in front of her. She widens her legs to invite me closer, like it's a position we've practiced a million times. The welcoming movement, combined with the way she's so comfortable in her skin around me, evokes a myriad of sinful thoughts. Truthfully, we haven't known each other long, but I have an ease with her that I've never had with anyone before—not even my ex. Her mouth forms a question and since I don't want her to delve into why I'm not the kind of guy her daddy would like, I ask, "How come you don't want kids? You said they weren't in your future."

Her lips compress and sadness moves into her eyes. I lean in to place a soft kiss on her mouth, tease her lips back open. I taste her sweetness and savor the flavor on my tongue, wanting to draw on it later when this summer affair is over.

"I'm a lawyer, and I'll be working eighteen-hour days," she explains, her voice tight.

"So it's not really that you don't *want* them. It's more like you're not going to have them because of your work commitments, right?"

"Yeah, I guess. I just . . . my parents are both lawyers, well, my mom was before she died."

"I'm sorry," I say quietly.

"Thank you. She's been gone a few years now, and I miss her like crazy, but when she was here, like Dad, she was pretty much absent my whole life. I don't ever want to bring a kid into the world and not be there for them, you know."

I stop breathing for a second, understanding she's telling me something very personal, something very close to her heart. "I can understand that," I say.

I move to her breasts and give a long slow lick over one nipple, then the other, needing her to relax again. I don't like seeing that wounded look in her eyes. Her purr resonates through my body and strokes my cock. It thickens another inch and presses hard against my zipper. I go back on my heels and unzip my pants to release the pressure.

I lean in again and run my lips along her throat. I catch the sweet scent of her arousal and breathe it into my lungs, unable to get enough of her. "Why did you follow in your parents' footsteps if you hate it so much?"

"What makes you think I hate it?" she asks, a tremble moving through her as I softly lick her earlobe. Jesus, I love the way her body reacts to me. She lets loose a breath and it flutters against my skin.

"When you told Gram you were a lawyer, your lips pursed like you'd just sucked a lemon." I place my hand on her throat to feel the way her body is humming with pleasure.

She chuckles, and the sweet sound covers me like a caress. Her hands move to my shoulders, and she touches me gently, traces a few of my deeper scars. "I had no idea I was so transparent." A tortured laugh catches in her throat. "That's not a great trait for a lawyer."

"So why did you go into law?" I press, wanting to know more, everything, about her, even though getting in too deep with the pampered rich girl goes against my own best interests. Everything I stand for. "Why did you do it, especially when you have such talent in design and it seems to be your true passion?"

She hesitates for a moment and looks down. I touch her shoulder to bring her attention back around to me. She tilts her head to meet my gaze and whispers, "It was expected of me."

I tuck a strand of hair behind her ear. "Do you always do what's expected of you?"

"Apparently. My father is a very controlling man. He hated the idea of me going into design. He said I'd never make it in the fashion business and that my designs weren't good enough."

Son of a bitch. My throat tightens to the point of pain, and I take a second to pull myself together before I hop on my bike and personally hunt the douchebag down. How could any fucking man—a father at that—so brutally shatter his little girl's dreams? I place my palm on her cheek and she leans into me, her body beckoning my touch.

"That's a pretty shitty thing to say. And for what it's worth, Kylee, he was wrong."

She gives me a sweet smile, but I get the sense she doesn't believe me or believe in herself. I guess that's the kind of thing that happens when you have no one to champion your true ambitions. I know all too well what that's like and from here on out, I'm going to show her she's good enough—better than good enough—and that *I* believe in her talent.

"I guess I'll never know," she whispers quietly

My heart aches for the girl desperate for approval. Maybe we have more in common than I ever thought. "My dad hated that I wanted to be a tattoo artist," I say, and I'm not sure if I'm doing it to console her or because I want to open up to her and share my pain too. "He was pretty shitty about it, I can tell you that. I was always a dreamer, and he hated that I lived in my head." My heart pinches as I think about my upbringing. Fuck, I miss my parents so much. "But you know what? He was always there for his family. He was a hard-ass son of a bitch, Kylee, but he was always there for his family." Even after I was accused of rape and thought he was going to beat the living shit out of me, he stood by my side.

"You guys are all there for each other," she says, her voice wistful, longing. "I love your family, Jamie. Summer was so lucky tonight." When her voice wavers, I glance up at her, and she puts her hands on my face, and her gaze searches mine. "You look tired," she says and brushes my hair back. "What time is it?"

"Late," I say. "But I'm never too tired for this." I dip my head and slowly drag my tongue over her pussy. Her body shudders at the first sweet touch of my tongue. She exhales a shuddery intimate laugh that catches in her throat as she relaxes into my touch. Finally. Her hands rake through my hair and she moves against my mouth. "I've been thinking about this moment all night," I say from between her thighs.

"Me too," she says. "I couldn't wait for you to get home."

Home.

This isn't home, Jamie. And this thing between you and Kylee, well, it's just sex. You've been down this road, don't set yourself up for disaster, by thinking this is more than it really is . . .

She continues to run her hand though my hair as I lick her pussy, and my blood pulses hotter. Her clit is hard, inflamed. "Have you been aching for my mouth here?" I ask and run my fingers over her wet sex. As I pet her lightly, she touches my arm, her fingers soft and hot on my skin. Warmth streaks through me, driving back the cold that resides inside me, hovering in my darkest corners. But, for self-preservation reasons, I keep that coldness close, a continual reminder of past mistakes.

"Yes," she admits, a strange new comfort between us as I take her slow, instead of fast and hard like I'd promised. Maybe I should go savage on her, ravage her hard and fast, because what I'm doing now, well, it feels an awful lot like lovemaking and scares the living shit out of me.

Working to keep my mind on the physical act only, I say, "Getting my mouth on you is all I've been able to think about."

"The girl wants that, too," she says. The teasing way she refers to herself as *the girl* is like a slap in the face, a wake-up call that this is sex and we're each playing a role. With that thought in mind, I work to keep a measure of emotional distance.

"The girl should have what the girl wants."

Her body flushes with color as I probe her wet opening, and she writhes and moans, her hands palming my shoulders and tugging me to her, like she can't get me close enough.

"I liked what we did on Skype, but it left me needing you," she admits.

"I wanted you so badly tonight," I say, needing to lighten my mood. "I nearly got caught rubbing one out in that damn supply closet," I say and laugh.

She chuckles, a sound mixed with humor and lust. "You are so bad, Jamie."

I push a finger inside her pussy and she clamps hard around me. I damn near fucking sob when I find her so hot, wet, and ready for me. Every. Single. Time. "I'd do it again though, if you wanted me to. I'd get into all kinds of trouble for you, Kylee."

"You were the one who called me." Her eyes light up, fill with laughter. "I was going along with you."

"Did you like it?" I wiggle my finger inside her and she groans.

"Yeah, I liked it."

Her pussy muscles grip me hard and my cock aches to get inside her heat. "Then I think you're as bad as me."

"More like you're corrupting me."

"Is that what you think I'm doing?" I ask as I roughly, greedily pull a nipple into my mouth. She groans and holds my head to her body, her erotic whimper stroking my dick.

"No, what I think you're doing is giving me the best sex of my life."

I grin at that, feeling a measure of smug satisfaction. I kiss her nipple and begin a slow descent, savoring the satiny warmth of her skin. My touch is slower this time, softer, less hurried. I reach her pussy and press my mouth hungrily into her sweetness. I deepen the kiss as I fuck her with my fingers. Her body shudders, so close to coming apart for me. I slow down, not ready to bring her over yet, not until my mouth has had its fill.

Like that's ever going to fucking happen.

She whimpers, her breathing harsh as her hips rock into me, moving, pressing, seeking what her body craves. As much as I want to be inside her, the desperate ache in my groin growing heavier, shrieking for relief, I have no intention of removing my mouth from her hot little cunt. Earlier tonight, just knowing I could come back here and put my mouth on her, lick her until she comes, is the only thing that got me through the long wait at the hospital.

I glance up and see the mesmerized look on her face as her gaze follows my every movement. "You like watching me lick you?"

She nods, completely open with me about her desires, and I fucking love that. No games, no inhibitions, just two people enjoying each other's bodies. As my world becomes her pleasure, I shift to give her a better look, but then I see her stand-up mirror in the corner. She cries out in distress when I slip out from between her legs, but when I reposition the mirror beside us so she can watch everything I'm doing to her, her groan becomes a moan of approval.

I angle her body, the explicit position completely exposing her, and press my fingers inside her as she props herself up on one elbow. She watches intently in the mirror, her eyes glassy, the ecstasy on her face filling me with a different kind of pleasure. Using long deep pushes, I slide my fingers in and out of her. Her muscles spasm, burn against my skin. The blood in my body practically ignites as her sweet sexy sounds urge me on, and she's so desperate for release now, I know I need to end the sweet torment.

I circle her clit with my tongue and lightly brush the hot bundle of nerves inside her. Her eyes go wide, her mouth slack, the need coming to a peak.

"Jamie," she whimpers, her composure slipping away as her body succumbs to the pleasure and lets go. Her hot juices drip down my hand and I bury my face in her gorgeous cunt. No fucking way am I missing a drop of her honey sweetness. I flatten my tongue and lick her, long lazy strokes from the bottom to the top and her thighs hug my head. I swear to fucking God, I could stay between her legs for an eternity and only come out when I need air. She gives a fluttery little breath when her body stops spasming, and I glance up at her, catch the way she's nibbling her lips.

"What?" I ask.

"I . . . want . . ." she begins but her words fall off. She touches my hair, pushes it from my face. What is going on in that beautiful mind of hers?

"Tell me what you want, Kylee, and I'll give it to you."

A pause and then, "Earlier, at the hospital, what you said . . ."

"About fucking your breasts," I run my hand over her hard nipples and she leans into me. "Then again, I talked about fucking this pretty mouth too." I slowly push a finger into her mouth and she runs her tongue over it. A wave of possessiveness swamps me, taking me by surprise, and I work diligently to breathe past it.

"I want all those things," she says, "But right now I want . . ."

Her voice falls off like she's still too embarrassed to tell me. After everything we've done, she has no need to be self-conscious and I won't have any of it.

"Say it," I whisper. "Don't hold back with me, ever."

She nods, sucks in a breath, and says, "I want to watch . . . you, like you did at the hospital. Then I want your cock in my mouth. I want to make you feel good, Jamie."

I slant my head. She wants to watch me, make me feel good? That's not at all what I expected her to say. "Yeah?" I ask, my voice lower.

"I want to watch you touch yourself." She gulps. "I know I saw it through Skype, but I want to see it here, now. And I want your cum, Jamie."

I love her openness and try to talk past the knot in my throat. "You liked that, did you?"

She nods, and the eagerness in her eyes excites me. "Well, I liked watching you, too. It was fucking hot." I push her hair from her face, take in her pretty pink blush. "You never have to ask for my cum. I want to fill you with it, everywhere."

She whimpers. "I want it everywhere, too," she says, need thickening her voice. "I want everything with you."

Yeah, and therein lies the problem because I want everything with her too. But that's a stupid thought, one I shouldn't be having. Not only is she leaving at the end of summer, when she finds out who I am and gets a whiff of my rap sheet, uncovers all my dirty secrets, this good girl is going to run a million miles in the opposite direction—and I don't blame her.

But those worries are for later, when she's not reaching for my jeans and shoving them to my thighs. I step back, make quick work of my pants, and grab my cock by the base. Desire grows in her eyes as her hand snakes out. She places it on my oblique muscles and my body trembles at her touch.

I move my hips, thrust hard into my hand, and she swallows hard as her hand follows the motions. The sound reverberates through my blood and fuels my hunger. Every nerve in my body comes alive as she watches me stroke my cock.

"I've never watched a man do this before," she says, and I

quickly close my eyes against the image of another man's hands on her body, desperate to dispel it.

She leans into me, and with each thrust forward, licks my crown. I shake my head, blindsided by lust and all the ways this woman pleasures me. Just when I thought sex with her couldn't get any better.

Fuck me.

I grip her hair and pull it back so I can see her pretty tongue. She laps at the pre-cum pooling on my slit and moans in delight. Fuck, she's just so goddamn perfect. She cups my balls, massages them gently, and they pull up into my body.

"Take me into your mouth," I say.

She rocks on the edge of the bed, and my cock hits the back of her throat. The sweet torture makes me throb. She whimpers, but the heat in her eyes as I catch our reflection in the mirror tells me it's from pleasure.

"That's it, Kylee. Take my cock into your throat. Let me know how much you like watching me rub my cock while I'm thinking about your hot pussy."

She widens her mouth and I power into her. Honest to fuck, the way she wants me, the way she is trying so hard to take me deep into her throat is a complete mind fuck. She relaxes her throat, takes me an inch deeper, and the erotic assault on my senses is too much for me to take. I don't want to lose control, it's too soon, but I can no longer hold off. I let loose a loud growl. I rock my hips, pleasure seeps from every dark corner, merges between my legs, and spills into her mouth. She gulps and swallows all of me, and my heart slams against my chest. Jesus, she's really something. She drinks all of me then grins up at me.

"Is that what the boy needed?" she asks.

I grin. "Yeah, is it what the girl needed?"

"Definitely," she murmurs, her look so sexy and sated, my cock twitches. I place a soft kiss onto her forehead and nudge her shoulders until she's flat out on the bed. I circle in, slide in beside her, and pull her close. Her body relaxes into mine, and when she gives a contented sigh, I pull her hair back and place a light open-mouth kiss onto her cheek. She cuddles into me, and warmth settles into my stomach as her soft moan wraps around us like a blanket. As we drift off to sleep I try not to think about how nice it was to know she was here waiting for me to come home, how I could so easily get used to falling asleep with her in my arms every night, or better yet, waking up with her each morning. But this is just an affair, nothing more—and I've got this.

Yeah right.

10

KYLEE

I stretch out on the bed, my body sore, hurting in hidden places that have rarely been used, or beautifully abused, before—but it's a good sore. My lids spring open as sweet memories of last night come rushing back in an erotic flash. Heat floods my veins, scorching through my body on its way to the needy juncture between my legs. I squeeze my thighs together and nearly bring on another orgasm. What have I become?

Honest to God, I can't believe I was brazen enough to ask Jamie to touch himself for me last night. But it was more than me just wanting him to "touch" himself. I actually asked him to masturbate while I watched, then took his beautiful cock down my throat as far as humanly possible—and then some. Everything we did last night, from the Skype sex to our coming together in the bedroom, was delightfully naughty and so out of character for me. This man is totally corrupting me, and I wouldn't have it any other way. Heat moves into my face as I relive the moment, but my blush isn't from embarrassment. No, it's from want. I want Jamie—again. I turn in the bed, and when I find the other side of the mattress empty, unease rushes through me.

I jackknife up and listen for sound. When I don't hear a circular saw or a hammer out on my back deck, I throw my legs over the side of the bed and listen for movement inside my cottage. My gaze strays to the clock and I shake my head. No wonder I'm so tired. It's barely the crack of dawn and Jamie and I hadn't settled in to sleep until the wee hours of the morning. My body warms again when I think about what kept us up so late.

Since it's Sunday and too early to work on the deck—no need to wake the vacationers who've already returned and have them pissed off at me—I tug on my robe and pad quietly through my chilly cottage. Had Jamie gotten up in the middle of the night and left, taken Scout back home, without so much as a goodbye? I know we're not dating, and we're not a couple who needs to check in with the other, but there is a part of me that wishes he had said goodbye, or . . . something. The cottage feels lonely without his presence, and as much as I hate to admit it, I feel a strange sense of emptiness.

Not good, Kylee, so not good.

I reach the kitchen and notice that Scout's bed is still in place, and the coffee in the pot hasn't reached its two-hour shut-off point yet. A note on the counter catches my eye and a little thrill goes through me.

Took Scout for a walk. Didn't want to wake you this early. Breakfast later?

I drop the note, pour a quick cup of coffee, and sip it as I hurry back to the bedroom, a little bubble of excitement welling up inside me. I dress in my running shorts and tug on a T-shirt. It's cold this time of the morning, but if I'm running, I'm going to work up a sweat so I don't bother with a sweater. I exit through the back screen door and think about resetting the alarm system but decide against it. Like

Jamie said, no one in Blue Bay ever locks their doors. My mind goes back to the creeped-out feeling I had last night, but I try to dispel it. I do have an overactive imagination—Lord knows my father berated me about it enough—but here in Blue Bay, the only danger the vacationers face is a rogue wave.

Or falling for Jamie.

I hurry outside and run toward the water, okay, more like speed walk, since I'm so freaking out of shape. My runners sink into the wet sand as the cool, salt spray falls over me. My hair tightens and coils like a damn Slinky on crack, compliments of the briny air. How attractive. I smooth the wayward strands down, but they frizz and stick together like Velcro. Giving up, I scan the distance, searching for signs of Jamie.

Deep in the morning mist, I see figures in the fog and head toward them. I pick up speed and try not to sound breathless as I make my way toward Jamie and Scout—yeah, I kind of want to pretend I jog on a regular basis—but once again, I suddenly get that eerie feeling that I'm being watched. I turn and sense a movement in the haze behind me. My heart jumps into my throat as I quickly assess the situation. This time I don't have a big scary dog at my side to frighten anyone away. With that thought in mind, I don't hang around to see who is going to emerge from the mist. Instead I take off full force down the beach.

I run, and I feel a measure of comfort when Jamie and Scout come into view. "Jamie," I cry out and wave, trying not to look or sound as frightened as I feel. He lets Scout go, and she darts toward me. She's running so damn fast, I try to slow myself down to get a hold of her leash but I get tangled up in it and fall face-first into the water as Scout barks and runs past me. Jamie hurries to me and drops to his knees.

"Jesus, Kylee, are you okay?" he slicks his damp hair off his forehead, and those gorgeous green eyes of his, the color of the ocean on a clear spring morning, move over my face and body with concern. My heart thumps. It's a little touching that he's so concerned.

I sputter as the cold Atlantic water races over me and chills me to the bones. "What's going on with Scout?" I ask as I try to pull myself out of the surf.

He looks up, glances past my shoulders, and frowns. "I don't know. She was whining early this morning. It woke me so I thought I'd take her for a walk. She seems spooked."

Do I tell him I'm spooked too? I mull that over and decide against it. It's likely just my overactive imagination. Lord knows Dad berated me enough over my "foolish musings," and it left me self-conscious, fearful of receiving skeptical glares and disapproving scowls. God, he really did a number on me.

"She's probably confused being at my place and missing Summer and Sean."

"Yeah, you're probably right."

He brushes my wet hair from my face, scoops me into his arms, and carries my soaked body to dry sand. He sets me down and I spit wet sand from my mouth as he sinks to his knees in front of me, his careful gaze moving over my face, assessing me.

Since the only thing hurt is my pride, I say, "I did that on purpose, you know. I hear an early morning mud bath is good for the skin."

"Oh, so you meant for this to happen?" He swallows and tries to avert his gaze, but not before I see his lips quirk at the corners.

"Are you laughing at me?" I shout and feign anger.

"No, not really."

"Not really?"

He cups my chin, his hand so warm against my flesh. "Did

anyone ever tell you how cute you look when you're mad and full of mud?"

"I'll have to take a nose dive into the surf more often, then. I had no idea that's how a girl goes about picking up a guy in Blue Bay."

His smile dissolves, and his muscles flex. "Kylee, I know we said one night, and we kind of blew that a few times." He pauses and scrubs his face.

Oh, I blew it all right. Literally and figuratively.

"Yeah . . ." I say, wanting him to continue.

"So I was thinking, maybe we could keep on doing what we're doing for the rest of the summer." He glances left, then right, like he's making sure the coast is clear and no one can hear him.

Sex with Jamie for a few more months.

I feel like I'm back in grade school with my hand in the air. Ooh, pick me, pick me.

When I don't readily respond he comes back with, "You don't have to answer me right away. Maybe you could give it some thought, though."

Thought? Nah, thoughts are overrated. "I could do that," I say quietly, not wanting to sound too damn eager, and the corner of his mouth curls as he bends forward and places the softest, gentlest kiss on my mouth. His rough scruff rasps over my skin, and my heart takes another tumble, a warning that this could be dangerous to me in so many ways.

"An affair with Jamie Owens, Blue Bay's very own bad boy. How naughty," I whisper into his mouth. "We should probably keep it quiet though. We don't want Gram thinking we're a couple, otherwise she'll—"

"Be at us to give her a great-grandbaby," he cuts in, but there is a strange look on his face, one that has me thinking he has other reasons for keeping things quiet.

Instead of asking—it's not like I don't have other reasons

too, one being my overbearing father—I say, "Right." A moment of silence, then, "So an affair, huh?" I add, more to myself than Jamie.

He angles his head, his look challenging. "Wasn't that what you were looking for that day you shook your sweet ass at me? A good girl out for a little fun with the local trouble-maker? Don't think I didn't know what you were up to."

God, I really am transparent. At least to him, anyway.

"Can't get anything by you, can I?"

His smile falters for a second, but then it's quickly back in place, showing those perfect white teeth of his. Speaking of teeth, mine are chattering like dice in a Yahtzee cup as I shiver almost uncontrollably, but the sound is muffled by Scout's distant growls.

"You . . . you better go get her," I say and hug myself to create heat. "And as far as your proposition goes, I've had enough time to think."

His eyes narrow in on me. "Tell me your answer is yes."

"Actually," I begin and he dips his head, his face strained. "That's a hell yes," I say, and his sexy grin returns. "Now go."

"You'll be okay to make it back to your house?"

"I'm a big girl," I say though chattering teeth. "I can take care of myself."

"Clearly," he says, that ridiculous sexy grin of his doing the dirtiest things to the greedy spot between my quivering legs. "Any girl who takes a cold mud bath at the crack of dawn must be tough."

"Tough, yeah, that's me," I say. I'm not.

He tugs off his shirt, and for a minute I forget everything. My God, he has such a beautiful body. "Take your shirt off and put this on," he says.

My head rears back, even though I'm touched by the gesture. "You want me to undress here, on the beach?"

"Yes, here. There is no one around to see you."

I look to my right, and Scout's growls go through me. "I'm not so sure about that," I say. "Scout is barking at someone."

"Or something. Don't worry. I'll deal with it. Right now you're freezing and you need to get warm before you get hypothermia. The ocean water is still too cold this time of year. Even for a mud bath," he adds, deadpan.

"Fine," I say gruffly and tug my shirt off. Jamie's gaze drops to my small breasts, and my pert nipples tighten even more. Oh, what I'd do to have that hot mouth of his wrapped around them again. "See something you like?" I ask teasingly, as I tug on his shirt and breathe in his scent. I let his distinct aroma curl around me, seep into my skin, warm my shivering body.

He smirks at me. "Yeah, I do," he responds unapologetically, and I keep the smile from my face. How is it this man makes me feel so desired? No man has ever fixated on my small breasts before, but Jamie, well, he looks at them like they're a prized possession, like they could win a first-place ribbon at the Blue Bay bake-off—or tits-off—if there's such a thing.

I'm going to fuck your tits.

As those dirty words ping around inside my brain, I gesture with a nod. "You better go find Scout."

"You sure you're okay?"

I climb to my feet, brush wet sand from my ass, and say, "Go. I'm fine."

"Head back to the house. I need to grab Scout some food from Sean's, then I'll meet you there."

I nod and he places another soft kiss onto my mouth, then runs down the beach after Scout. He calls out to Scout and his voice echoes through me as I grab my wet shirt and head to higher ground. I reach the string of cottages over-looking the ocean and walk in the sand as I pass. Most of the places are still empty this early in the season, but I see a light on inside one of the more luxurious homes. Nosy girl that I am, I try to peek into the window as I hurry past it, but slow my steps when I come to Summer's quaint cottage. Just then Jamie and Scout emerge from the fog and I let loose a relieved breath.

"Thank God you found her." My gaze falls over Jamie, his naked chest to be precise, and a fine shiver moves through me. I swear to God, I really did win the man lottery with this one. Truthfully, I can't believe he's asking for a summer fling. I agreed, but deep down I'll have to be careful. When I head back to Atlanta come September, I have to make sure I don't leave my heart in Blue Bay.

"She was at the other end of the beach, chasing the seagulls." A sound lodges in his throat and he grimaces as I stand there shivering "Jesus Christ, Kylee, you're freezing," he says, the worry in the depths of his voice wrapping around my heart and tugging tight. "You need to get out of these wet clothes. Come here." He puts his arm around me and pulls me tight against his body. I sink into him, absorb his heat. "Let's get you inside while I grab Scout's food."

He pulls a key from his shorts and opens the door. Scout darts in ahead of us and goes wild as she sniffs and races from room to room. At first I don't think it's odd, considering she did the same thing when I brought her to my cottage.

"I think she's missing her mom and dad," I say, but Jamie frowns. "What?" I ask.

"Did you leave the light in the kitchen on last night?"

A shiver of unease moves through me. Is it possible that Scout is picking up the scent of an intruder? I glance down and rack my memory. Last evening, I hightailed it out of here with Scout so fast, I don't remember. Before I can answer, he says, "When I drove by last night, I could have sworn the lights were all off."

"I can't remember, Jamie. I might have left it on. Do you think someone broke in?"

He walks through the house and I follow him. "Nothing's missing, so I don't think so. You probably just forgot, and I was tired coming home." He goes to the pantry and grabs Scout's food, then stops. "Wait, you don't mind if Scout stays at your place, do you?"

I grin at him and wet my bottom lip, a vicious tease. "As long as it's a package deal," I say and walk up to him. His eyes go dark, full of hunger as he pulls me to him. His T-shirt is slightly damp and cold—my skin was wet when I pulled it on—but he doesn't seem to mind as it presses against his naked chest.

"We need to get you home and warmed up," he murmurs into my mouth, and my legs nearly buckle at the desire I hear in his voice.

"Any idea on how we can do that?" I ask.

"Plenty."

He grabs Scout's food and I reach for her leash when she finally comes back into the front room. Jamie sets the alarm and we head outside.

"I thought you said people here didn't even lock their doors?"

"Summer had some trouble a while back, so Sean asked me to install a system."

"Really, you installed it?" I ask and look him over. There is so much more to this man than he lets on.

"Yeah, when I was living in New Orleans, I worked for a company called Eagle Security."

"Then you got into the tattoo business."

"It was a hobby that led to a career," he says.

"Why did you come back to Blue Bay?"

He kicks a pebble and it echoes in the quiet of the morning. Scout barks at it, and I rub her head to hush her. Only problem is, I get a big wet tongue across the face when I bend.

"Ugh, like I'm not wet enough," I say and Jamie quirks a brow, his dirty mind clearly at work. "From falling into the water," I say and give him a little push. He doesn't budge. Cripes, I'd have more luck moving a tree with my pinkie than I would moving two hundred pounds of hard muscle with a shove. "So why did you come back, Jamie?" I ask, getting the conversation back on track, curious about this man. The truth is I hate how interested I am. I should rein in my curiosity, but I can't seem to. I want to know more, what makes him tick.

"Because my brother Sean made me. After Dad died, he called us all home to help get Dad's construction business back in the black. We were all expected to drop whatever it was we were doing and hightail it back here."

"Do you always do everything that's expected of you?" I say and grin as I toss his words back at him.

"Apparently. The thing is, all of us guys left the first chance we could." He frowns and looks down, but I don't miss the demons dancing in his eyes before he blinks them away.

"How come?" I pry, even though it's not my business.

He gives an easy shrug, but that's a difficult task when you have something weighing your shoulders down, and that's exactly what I think is going on with him. I understand his secrets don't involve me, but the fact that he wants to keep our relationship incognito does. Why is he so afraid of anyone finding out?

"We all had our own reasons," he says, then a sound catches in his throat. "Dad mostly."

"I know he was hard on you, but was that your reason, too?" I ask, and he goes stiff beside me.

"I had to find myself. Figure out my life," he mutters and

scrubs his hand over his chin. The sound rasps through my body and brings on a shiver. He clearly misreads the reaction and drags me closer, warming me with his heat. I love the feel of his body next to mine, so I don't correct him.

"And that happened in New Orleans? You found yourself there?"

He turns to me, and his steely eyes lock on mine. "I'm not sure it's happened yet, Kylee."

We go quiet for a long time, both lost in our own thoughts as we listen to the savage surf lap against the sandy shore. I break the quiet and say, "Well, if I grew up here, I'd never leave. Everything here just seems so much more . . . simple."

"Lots of reasons to leave, and lots of reasons to come back." His hair falls forward as he angles his head my way. "Blue Bay is in my soul, and we can all kid ourselves by saying we only came back because Sean made us, but this place sort of grips you . . ." He pauses and makes a fist. ". . . By the balls and holds you here."

"Poetic," I say and nudge him, and while I sound like I'm kidding, I'm not. Underneath the tattoos and scars there is a whole other side of Jamie. "It is beautiful here."

"Yeah, beautiful," he says, and I feel a flush move into my cheeks when I realize he's talking about me.

We reach my place and I open the door. "So you don't think there was anyone on the beach?"

He brushes my wet hair from my face, his dark gaze locked on mine. "No, why?" he asks.

For a minute I think about telling him I thought I saw someone, but I'm not really sure if I did. I think maybe I've watched too many horror movies and my imagination got carried away in the fog. Dad always scolded me for it, but would Jamie? I don't think he would.

"Oh, just wondering."

"What's going on, Kylee?"

I hesitate for a long moment, but I'm comfortable with this man, and everything in me tells me he wouldn't laugh or make fun of me. "I don't know. I thought I saw someone, I guess."

His eyes narrow, concern on his face. "All I saw were seagulls," he says, but I hear a hint of worry lacing his voice. "Want me to go back and check?"

I appreciate the gesture so much my heart warms, and it puts me at ease. "No, I'm sure it's just my imagination getting the better of me." He hesitates for a second, and I squeeze his arm. "Seriously, it's fine."

"Okay, why don't you get rinsed off while I take care of Scout?"

"After you take care of Scout, why don't you build a fire, then meet me in the shower? I think I have sand packed in places I can't reach."

Jamie laughs and I can't help but laugh with him. "Now there's an offer a guy can't refuse. Should I bring my jackhammer?"

Needy girl that I'm becoming—compliments of Jamie Owens—I reach down and cup his cock through his running shorts. It grows in my hand and he jerks his hips forward. "If by jackhammer, you mean your cock, then yes."

He reaches behind me, slaps my ass, and says, "Go. I'll take care of Scout, make a fire, and meet you in the shower. Don't start without me."

With my ass stinging from his slap, I hurry down the hall, stripping off my wet clothes as I go, and head straight for the shower. Dog food fills the bowl in the other room, and the sound of paper crinkling reaches my ears as I stop to look at myself in the mirror. I nearly scream at the horrific image staring back. My hair sticking out in all direction, and I have mud all over my face. Jamie found this attractive? Then again, he could be tarred and feathered and wearing a burlap bag and I'd find him attractive—because I like who he is. Could Jamie feel the same about me? Is he attracted to me for more than my face and body? Do I dare hope? I shake my head to clear it. What would that matter anyway? His life is here and I'm leaving in a few short months.

For God's sake, get it together, Kylee.

I turn the water on and hop in the warm spray. It feels glorious against my cold body, but once again my thoughts stray.

I'm not the kind of guy a girl brings home to Daddy.

Why would he say that? He's perfect in so many ways. Then again, I can't imagine ever bringing him home. He's not the "type" of guy my dad would want me with. I scoff. No doubt he'd do a full background check and dig up as much dirt on the guy as possible. I'd never want to put Jamie, or any man, through that. Sometimes, I swear to God, my father keeps a trace on me and tracks my every movement. I suck in a quick breath. Maybe someone *is* watching me here in Blue Bay. Maybe Dad did send one of his secret informants here to make sure I ride the straight and narrow.

Is it possible?

The shower door slides open and all my thoughts dissipate, all except one—Jamie—and the way he looks at me. He steps inside, crowds me with his big, powerful body. He's rough and ready—an impenetrable force. That's my Jamie. But then there are his scars, a contradiction, and a reminder that he's breakable like the rest of us.

He slides his hands around my shoulders and grips my neck. I gasp at the way he makes me feel so needed. Holding me tight, he bends and lightly presses his lips to mine. The kiss feels far more tender, far more personal, than any before it. I step into him until our naked bodies are touching, skin on skin, flesh on flesh. His hands slide down my back, a soft caress along my vertebrae, and I sway against him. Needy, so damn needy.

His stiff cock presses against my abdomen, and I move my body to massage him. His soft growls seep through me and twist me up inside. "Are you warming up?"

"I am now," I say, compliments of his heat, not the hot spray, pushing back the cold and warming my bones.

He touches my shoulders and eases me away from him. His hot gaze moves down my body, an explicit caress that stops when it reaches the juncture between my legs. "I fucking love looking at you." I swallow against the sudden dryness in my mouth, and he reaches for the soap. "Let me clean you."

He lathers his hands and puts them on my body, his touch so gentle and caring, my heart beats triple-time. "What are your plans for the day?" he asks, like showering together and making conversation is part of our normal routine. I sway against him, the closeness I feel to him right now, this very second, completely overwhelming me.

"I wouldn't mind seeing the baby, if Summer is up to it. Do you know if she'll be home today?" I'd also like to take a trip into Hope Falls and drop off some of my handmade clothes to little Katrina and her mother, but I don't bother telling him that. It's just something I want to do for them, no strings, no glory needed. Unlike my father's motives where charities are concerned, mine are altruistic. I just want to do something nice for a family that is struggling.

"She'll likely be discharged today." His soapy hands run over my shoulders and breasts, and he slides them along the underside to scrub away the sand. His fingers, big and protective, skate over my flesh, and arousal pulses through my veins. I glance at his large hands, the way they are taking care of me, making me feel so little in comparison to this massive guy. He might be lethal, but I don't feel the least bit afraid of him.

"Is this supposed to be turning me on?" I ask on a breathless whisper.

Instead of answering, he grips my shoulders and turns me away from him. He takes my hands in his and puts them on the wall. He pushes his knee between my legs to spread them.

"Stay like this for me. I need you wide open so I can wash every inch of you," he says, his voice deeper, harsher, like he'd just swallowed a handful of the gritty sand he's trying to rinse from my body.

"Okay," I say, willing to do just about anything this man wants me to, as long as he keeps touching me.

"If you want, before I start working on the deck, I can take you to Gram's to see Summer and the baby when they get home." He pushes my wet hair forward and it falls over my breasts, the wet strands sticking to my soaped-up nipples.

"Thanks, but I can take my own car. I have some . . . things to do." His hands still for a second. "Plus we probably shouldn't be seen together so much, right? We don't want anyone to get the wrong idea."

"Yeah," he says and resumes touching me—thank God—and runs his rough hands down my back and over my ass cheeks.

"But I'd like for you to be there at the same time," I say. "All your brothers and cousins in the same place can be a bit intimidating."

"You have nothing to be afraid of. They'd never touch you, and if anyone tried anything you didn't like, they'd have me to deal with."

"I take it no one messes with your girl." As soon as the words leave my mouth I realize what I've said. "I mean—"

"Can you go up on your tiptoes for me, Kylee?" he asks, and his hot breath falls over me, a soft sultry caress on my skin.

I quake. Hard. And do as he asks. I go up on my toes and

he drops to his knees, the hot spray hitting his back. He runs his hands over my cheeks, and then slides his fingers in between. Oh, my. His lips graze over my skin, and I whimper when he cups my cheeks and spreads them. Never in my life have I felt so exposed, open. I seize up a little and lean against the wall, away from him.

"It's okay," he whispers. "I've got you." Working diligently to relax, I suck in a breath and let it out slowly. His thumb presses into my opening and I splay my fingers on the wall and whimper, anxiety overcoming me.

"Jamie . . ." I murmured.

"You trust me, Kylee?" he asks, obviously picking up on the uncertainty in my voice.

I think about that for a moment. I *do* trust him. I've known a lot of men in my life, but I would never trust them the way I trust this man.

"Yes," I say quietly.

"Then will you put your body in my hands? Trust that I'll take care of it?"

My body instantly relaxes as I hand myself over to him completely. Deep down I know I'm in the right hands, know that never in a million years would he hurt me physically. Emotionally, well, that's a different story—and the fault would be mine, not his. I know the score where Jamie is concerned.

"My body is yours, Jamie," I whisper.

"Good, because Kylee, I *have* to touch you everywhere. It's not a want, it's a need."

I turn to see him. His face looks harsh, tortured, and it strips me bare inside. I've never had a man want me the way he does. I take a breath, but it's difficult to fill my quivering lungs.

"Take me," I say and turn back around, my throat tight,

my body humming, eager for anything and everything he's willing to give me.

He applies gentle pressure to my opening, taking such good care of my body, and I relax into his touch. He doesn't enter very far, just enough to let me know he's there. I take a deep, hitching breath, surprised I don't hate it. The truth is, I *need* him to touch me everywhere too.

"You feel me?"

"Yes."

"You've never been fucked here, have you?" he asks.

"No. I . . . I haven't really been with a lot of men," I admit and it seems to do something to him, bring out a softness in his touch.

He runs his palm along my back, a light, barely there caress. "I won't hurt you, Kylee. I'd never hurt you."

"I know."

"I'm going to go a little deeper," he says, and he wiggles his finger until I feel full, swollen, lush, and completely aroused. "I won't take you here until you're ready and begging for it." He stills inside me, letting me get used to explicit invasion. He pulls out and gently eases back in again as his other hand curls around my body and brushes over my clit. He strokes me, deeply, and circles my clit, coming perilously close but never touching. I'm instantly on the edge, seduced by a man who can make me orgasm simply by looking at me.

"Please," I beg and move my hips back and forth, eager for him to do something, anything. But no, he just keeps one finger in my ass and one circling my clit, like a predatory bird closing in on its prey. He chuckles again and I want to murder him for taking me high and leaving me hanging.

He removes his fingers from my body, and I want to scream. "There we go," he says, his voice a quiet whisper. "No more sand in that hard-to-reach place. You can go back on your heels now."

I fall back, and for a minute I wonder if her really needed me on my tiptoes or he just wanted my backside tipped up in the air for his personal viewing. I'm starting to believe he's an ass man. I grin and store that information away for later. After all, we now have all summer to play with each other. I have a few ideas for how I can make him as crazed as he always makes me.

"Actually," I say. "I think there is one more hard-to-reach place you missed."

His chuckle curls around me as he takes his time with me, no hurry to pounce like he has in the past. His mood is different, relaxed—Jamie unwound. I like this side of him every bit as much as I like Jamie unleashed.

"Patience, Kylee," he breathes into my ear, his hot breath sliding across the outer shell and massaging my arousal. "I never said I was finished."

His hands span my waist as his hard cock presses against my lower back. He rocks into me, slowly, softly, like he's savoring my body, drawing out the seduction. But I need it now, dammit.

"Jamie, please . . ." As fire licks over my thighs and a restless ache tugs at every muscle, I'm not above begging for what I need. Hard and fast is one thing, but this . . . this slow seduction, the way he's slowly, sweetly reacquainting his hands and mouth with my body, is damn near killing me.

He turns me to face him, and his eyes are the deepest shade of green I've ever seen. He dips his head, brushes his mouth over my eyes, nose, cheeks, and mouth. Big hands slide down my body, and needy girl that I am, I widen my legs to let him know exactly where I need him. He runs his finger over my outer lips, and it sends a blast of heat through me.

"Yes," I murmur.

"Is this where you need to be touched, Kylee?"

I rock into him, answering his question, and he inserts a

finger. My sex muscles tremble around it and I move my hips to grind my clit against his palm. I gasp as the dual combination shuts down my ability to think with any sort of clarity.

"That feels so good." I'm so close my body is trembling like a leaf in a windstorm. I grip his shoulders to hang on, but he pulls his fingers from me and spins me around again. His strong arms circle my waist to hold me as he gently pushes on my shoulders to bend me forward.

"Hands on the wall," he orders softly as he repositions me.

I take deep gulping breaths and brace my hands on the wall, knowing what's coming next and beyond excited for it. I've never been this soaking wet, this urgent to have a man's hands and mouth on me—his cock inside me. He anchors my body and rubs his cock over my ass before he slowly slides it into my hot sex. One glorious inch at a time, and damned if he doesn't have so many glorious inches to give. I stop breathing, stop moving, and he leans over me to press hot kisses to my nape.

"Breathe, Kylee," he murmurs, and the second I suck in a breath he pushes all the way inside me.

"Oh, my God," I say, and exhale harshly as my sex muscles clench around his long, thick length.

He pulls out and slides back in again, his rhythm slow and sweet as he takes me deeply, penetrating both my body and my soul.

Careful, Kylee.

"You feel fucking amazing," he murmurs.

He stays still inside me, neither of us in a hurry to move or break apart. Pleasure boils the blood in my veins and I gulp. Jamie asked for a summer of sex, but this feels like so much . . . more. In fact it feels intensely real. Deeply intimate. I crane my neck to see him, and his mouth closes over mine. He kisses me with such need and passion, by the time he breaks it we're both panting.

He inches out only to push back into me, slowly, giving me an inch at a time as his hands race over my body, pulling and tugging like he can't get enough, can't get me close enough. I give in to him, let him own me, take everything he needs. But Jamie isn't a man to take without giving, and right now, he's giving me everything he has and then some.

We rock, and my vision fades as barbed pleasure centers between my legs. He changes his angle, and his cock hits my G-spot with precision. I scratch at the tiled wall, and hiss, "Jamie," I cry, and he reaches around me to tap my clit, bringing on an explosive orgasm. I shake, pant, quiver all over, and my knees buckle as my hands slip on the wall, but Jamie has a good grip around my waist so I don't fall.

"Jesus fuck," he says. "You're so hot on my dick." His body tenses behind me as he grips my hips for leverage and depletes himself inside me. His breath scorches my skin as he hugs me to him. His hand moves over my back, tracing my vertebrae and taunting me all over again. He grips my hair and strokes it, his ragged breath evening out, slowing down.

His throat sounds as he swallows. "You good?"

"I'm good," I whisper, hating how much I love the way he checks in on me, that he cares about my well-being, even though this is just about sex.

"Come here." He turns me, and I lay my head on his chest, feel his powerful heartbeat beneath my cheek. He shifts me and puts me under the warm spray. The water falls over me and feels glorious against my skin. "I didn't miss any of those hard-to-reach places, did I?" he says, his voice full of humor.

"I believe you got all those hard-to-reach places and then some."

He laughs, but it falls off when I trace one of his deeper scars. I glance up at him, examining the eagle-shaped scar on his jawline. "What are these scars from, Jamie?"

A dark fierceness moves into his eyes. "From a long time ago." His jaw clenches and I get the sense I hit on something sensitive, something he has no intention of talking about. My heart hurts for him and whatever incident he found himself in that cut him so deeply, on the surface and below it.

Deciding to change the subject, I trace a few designs. "Have you ever been serious with anyone?"

"Once, a long time ago." he says his deep, hard voice rumbling though me. "You?"

"No." I think about telling him about Trevor, and how my dad wants me to marry him, but stop myself. I could never marry a man like that. No, if I were ever to get married—which I don't see happening anyway—it would be to a guy who was sweet, caring, protective, and cared about me for me, not for who my family was. Where on earth would I ever find a guy like that? I glance up at Jamie and when he smooths my hair back and drops a soft kiss onto my forehead, my heart hitches. It's insane how that intimate kiss felt more personal than when he was inside me. I squeeze my eyes shut to harden myself. We've set boundaries, and I know better than to cross them.

So not an easy task with Jamie.

"How come you never put her name on your body?"

"Ink is permanent. Relationships aren't."

I flinch at the harshness in his voice and put my head under the hot spray as his cold words chill me. "I don't know about that. Look at Summer and Sean. They seem pretty permanent."

"That's because Summer and Sean go way back. She's one of us."

"One of us?"

"A local. Not some out-of-towner."

"Oh," I say and put my face under the spray to hide the things I shouldn't be feeling. I get it. No matter who I am or

what I do, I will never be anything other than a summer vacationer, someone to have sex with, but not marriage material. I
turn from Jamie, totally pissed off at myself. I'm not looking
for marriage from him, anyway. I was just wondering if he
ever had anyone special. I knew what I was getting into when
I agreed to a summer fling and should delight in the tempo-
rariness of it all. I'm not in the market for more and these
stupid emotions are coming out of nowhere. Then again, they
could be a reaction to his gentle lovemaking and the way he
took care of me.

Lovemaking?

No, it was just sex. Amazing, mind-blowing sex. But sex
nonetheless

11

JAMIE

It's mid-afternoon by the time I cut and toss the last rotten pieces of the wood into the metal garbage bin and call it quits for the day. I brush my hands on my jeans and remove my tool belt. I'm hot and sweaty and thinking about jumping into the ocean when my cell phone pings. I pull it from my back pocket and slide my hand over the screen to see a text from Sean.

We're home.

Foregoing a swim, I hurry inside and jump in the shower. As I quickly rinse off I try not to think about all the things I did in here earlier with Kylee. Sweet Kylee, who put herself in my hands and felt so good wrapped around my cock. My dick thickens as I think about her, but I tamp it down. I really do not need a motherfucking boner when I go to Gram's.

Kylee said she had some errands to run and had packed a duffle bag. Shit, if I didn't know better, I'd think she was going somewhere overnight. Then again, I don't know better, do I? But I didn't ask where she was going, and she didn't supply the information. What she does in Blue Bay is her business, right? And the fact that she didn't bother telling me shouldn't make me feel this shitty. She has no reason to check in with me. I'm not her boyfriend. I'm her summer fuck buddy. We made that clear from the beginning.

I rinse off, towel dry, and reach into my bag for some clean clothes. I'd packed with the intention of staying at Sean's for the week, so I could take care of Scout while they were at the hospital and then at Gram's, but my plans had obviously changed.

I step into the main room and find Scout on her bed, her tail thumping when she sees me. "Hey girl, want to go for a walk?"

She jumps up and her nails scratch the wood floor as she races to the door. Like I even had to ask! I follow her, grab her leash, and step back outside. We make our way to the water, and I jog slowly as she keeps close to my heels. Off in the distance, I scan the cottages lining the sand, looking for anything or anyone that might have spooked Kylee. I hate that she was afraid, but as long as she's with me, she has nothing to fear. I'd never let any harm come to her. My gaze strays, and my stomach clenches when I hear a car door slam and see activity at the old Jackinoff cottage.

Son of a fucking bitch.

Had the place changed hands without my knowledge, or has one of the asshole brothers returned to Blue Bay? If it's the latter, he'd better stay the fuck away from me. Nothing good could come from us running into each other. As anger prowls through my blood, I rub my jawline, trace my scar, and my feet come to a resounding halt. What if it's not one of the asshole brothers, but my ex herself? I swallow down the bile punching into my throat. I'd hoped to never set eyes on her again, but there was a part of me that knew in returning to Blue Bay there could be a chance our paths would collide. My mind races back to my meeting with Walker at Summer's baby shower. It seemed to me he knew something I didn't. Could this be it?

"Let's go, Scout," I say and turn back around. My feet sink into the sand, my shoulders feeling heavier than moments ago as we make our way back to Kylee's place, a sick knot in my stomach as old, painful memories come racing back.

I unhook her, give her water, and lock up on my way out. But as I put the key into my pocket, the hairs on my arm prickle. The Jackinoff brothers are assholes, yes. But surely they wouldn't have broken into Sean's place looking for dirt that will put one of us away or drive us out of town—yeah, the law is always on the side of the rich vacationers. I shake my head. Kylee must have left the lights on. Otherwise there's going to be hell to pay.

My tires spin as I peel out of the driveway and head into town. I drive down Main Street, and before I pass through the hub, Indigo Blue, a store across from Benny's Groceries, catches my eye. As an idea forms, one that could either totally piss Kylee off or make her the happiest girl in the world, I pull the truck over, park it, and make my way inside the boutique. Overstepping boundaries? Yeah, probably.

Twenty minutes later, I'm back in my truck and on my way out of town again. The old homestead rises up in the distance as I turn down the lane. I glance around, take in all the trucks and bikes, but Kylee's car is nowhere to be found. Where the hell did she go?

I kill the ignition and take the steps two at a time. I enter the house to find my brothers and cousins all fussing around Summer and the baby, while Sean beams with pride.

"He looks like you, Sean," I say as I glance at the little boy in Summer's arm.

Tyler shakes his head. "Poor kid."

I grin at my baby brother. "It could have been worse. He could have looked like you."

Ty rubs his chin and lifts it a little higher. "Why is everyone so jealous of this pretty face?"

I scoff. "Pretty. I've seen prettier faces on the ass end of a donkey."

Tyler jumps to his feet, and within seconds he has me in a rear naked chokehold and is cutting off my air supply. "Tap out, big brother," he says.

"Like hell." I twist and turn, but would rather be rendered unconscious than give in to Tyler.

We stumble around the kitchen, and when a knock sounds on the door, Tyler turns toward it, with me still stuck in a hold. The second I see Kylee standing on the stoop, her expression nervous, I jab Tyler in the ribs. Fucker better let me go, or he's going to be sorry.

"Cut it out you two. Gram is trying to sleep. She stayed at the hospital with us last night," Summer says.

Ty lets me go, and I instantly throw my arm around his neck and give him a noogie. I rub my knuckles against his skull and mess up his hair. "You bastard," he says, and Sean gives me a shove. I let my baby brother go, and he punches me in the arm, a loving brotherly punch, but it hurts like a bitch. The guy can fucking hit. I wouldn't want to come up against him in a cage, that's for fucking sure.

I turn to Kylee whose eyes are as big as softballs, but fucking Jared cuts in front of me to let her in. I'm ready to tell him to back the fuck off, but since Kylee and I are "secretly" fucking, I don't. Can't imagine what Sean would say if he knew what I was up to. He saw firsthand what I went through after getting involved with the wrong girl last time and would no doubt kick my ass.

But is Kylee the *wrong* girl?

Kylee steps in and her gaze moves over mine before turning to Summer. She makes a squealing sound when she sees little Devon, and her knuckles brush mine as she passes me. I don't know if the touch was on purpose or not but I feel it all the way to my dick.

I plunk down into one of the empty chairs and glance around the room. Ty goes to the fridge for a drink as cousin Jace, a former chef in New York, checks on the pot roast cooking in the oven. With Gram resting, I guess he's cooking Sunday dinner. He's the only one she'll let in the kitchen with her, but come tomorrow she'll likely shove him out and be back at her beloved stove. The twins, Jared and Jacob, grab seats to my left, and my other cousins Ryan and Carter are in the family room, watching a baseball game on TV. I want to ask the guys if they know if any of the Jacki-noff brothers are back in town but won't do it while Kylee is here.

My attention zeroes in on Kylee when she sits next to Summer and takes Devon into her arms. Her eyes are watery as she looks at the baby with longing. For a girl who says kids aren't in her future, she's gazing at Devon like a woman in love.

"He's precious," she says.

"See what he's wearing." Summer opens the blanket, and Kylee sniffs when she sees he's wearing the cute baby outfit she made for him. "It fits him great. You really should be selling your designs."

Kylee nods, but doesn't say anything else. It's like she's pretty much resigned herself to the fact that her clothes aren't saleable, which is total bullshit. Her father really did a fucking number on her. When little Devon starts fussing, she looks a bit panicky and glances at Summer for help.

Summer laughs and takes him from her. "The boy can eat. Every two hours."

Kylee shakes her head. "You must be exhausted."

"I am."

"Is there anything I can do to help?"

"You helped with Scout last night, and I really appreciate it."

"Actually she's at my place sleeping right now."

Something sparks in Summer's eyes. "Oh?"

"I brought her with me while I worked on the deck," I pipe in. "I didn't want to leave her at your place alone." Not a lie.

"You don't mind?" Summer asks Kylee.

She shakes her head. "I love dogs. I always wanted one as a kid but . . ." She goes stiff like she's said too much. "A dog just didn't fit into our family, is all."

"Well, while you're in Blue Bay, consider my dog your dog."

Kylee gives Summer a warm smile, and my heart pinches for the little girl who was denied a dog. We had Bear growing up. A great big Labrador retriever. He was the best dog in the world and a kid who doesn't know the love of a dog, understand the bond, is a kid who missed out on a lot.

Summer puts her hand over Kylee's. "If you don't have any plans, why don't you stay for supper?"

"I . . . sure. I can help cook. I feel like I need to be doing something useful."

"You don't have to, but if you want to help Jace, I'm sure he'd appreciate it."

Jace slides Kylee a look, his dimples prominent as he grins at her. "I'd never say no to a pretty woman in the kitchen with me."

A blush crawls up Kylee's neck and she steals a glance my way. I look her over and my gaze moves to Summer as she winks at me and says, "The rest of the guys are pretty useless in the kitchen."

"Hey, I take offense to that," I say, while the other guys nod in complete agreement with her.

"Come on, Jamie. You're useless in the kitchen. You wouldn't know a spatula from a can opener."

I grin at her. "There are things I can do in the kitchen with a spatula," I say and she rolls her eyes at me.

"Things I don't want to hear about," she shoots back and laughs as she stands. "I think I'll feed this little one and take a nap before dinner."

"I'll join you," Sean says, and puts his arm around his wife to lead her upstairs. I smile as I watch them go, an invisible band squeezing my heart when I see how happy my brother is, the tender way he's taking care of his family.

His family.

I suddenly long for my own, and that scares the shit out of me, because I'll never have what Sean and Summer have. Those two go way back and belong together. It was years in the making but both of them are exactly where they need to be.

"Let's go for a ride," Jacob says to his twin, Jared. "I just changed the jetting on my bike and want to give it a good run."

As the twins leave to give their dirt bikes a run, Kylee stands. "What can I help you with, Jace?" she asks. She moves in next to my cousin and stands close, too close. As they talk about the meal, the sudden vision of Kylee in the arms of another fills me with anger and jealousy, and I fist my hands, wanting to punch something or someone.

"Come on bro, let's go watch the game," Ty says and puts his hand on my shoulder.

"Yeah, okay." Kylee's eyes flash my way as I turn, leaving her alone with my cousin, a guy who has no idea Kylee's my girl. Yeah, she's my fucking girl. At least for the summer, anyway.

I plunk down onto the sofa, and from where I'm sitting I can see my girl in the kitchen. I watch her for a few moments, then my thoughts race back to the Jackinoff brothers.

"Hey," I say to the guys. "There's action at the Jackinoff cottage. You guys know anything about that?"

"No fucking way," Ryan says, and turns my way, his gaze murderous.

"Have you heard anything?" I ask. I lean forward and brace my elbows on my knee. I don't want Kylee to overhear our conversation. I figure the rumors will reach her ears soon enough. The thing is, the longer I keep the truth from her, the harder it is. It's not that I'm lying to her. Then again, is omission the same as lying? What will happen when she finds out? Will she believe me, believe in me, or run the other fucking way? The more I get to know her the less I want her to run the other way, which boils down to this—I'm nervous as fuck, praying she never finds out.

Carter shakes his head. "No, nothing. Want me to drive by, pay them a visit?"

Tyler cracks his knuckles, his face that of a stone-cold fighter. "Yeah, I'll go with you."

"No, let's wait and see. Could be nothing."

There's a moment of silence as all three guys stare at me, then they turn back to the game. From the kitchen a cell phone rings, and Kylee rushes to her purse. She pulls out her phone and stares at it a second, her nose crinkled. Is she not going to answer it? She slides her finger across the screen and her words are hushed as she darts outside for privacy. For a second I wonder who she's talking to. Someone she'd met up with earlier today? Possessiveness races through me and I try to push it back, rein it in, but it's useless. The idea of her with another man sits like a fireball in my gut.

When Jace darts to the bathroom, I push from my chair and, under the guise of getting a drink, step into the kitchen. I can hear Kylee talking outside. I want to give her privacy, I really do, but the anxiety in her voice worries me. I step up to the open window and hear her shaky words.

"Not, it's not that. I've just been busy."

I listen to the one-sided conversation and instantly get the sense that it's her father.

"I'm on vacation. What does it matter what I'm doing with my time?" A pause and then. "I have been texting him back."

Texting who back?

White-hot jealousy prowls through my blood.

"Okay, yes." I look out the window and catch the way she's pinching the bridge of her nose. "Yes, I understand that is the nicest office," she says. "Best view of the city, I know." A few more words are exchanged and she comes back into the kitchen, the screen door banging behind her.

She goes still, her eyes wide when she sees me standing at the sink. "Hey," she says.

"I wasn't trying to listen," I fib. "I just wanted to make sure you were okay."

"I'm okay."

I pitch my voice low, and I want to ask who it was she texted back but is it any of my business? Not really. "Are you sure?"

"Yeah, I'm sure," she says, her voice light, but the act is wasted on me. I can see beneath it. Something's bothering her.

"Sounds like your father is upset."

She nods. "I haven't been checking in."

"He definitely keeps close tabs on you."

She frowns. "I know. I appreciate that he cares, you know? But sometimes it's too much, and I'm tired of him pressuring me . . ." Her voice falls off.

"Pressuring you? How?"

She throws her hands up in the air. "Work, my personal life . . . everything."

I dip my head and lower my voice even more. "Does your father know about me?"

"Oh, God no!" she says quickly. "I would never tell him—" Her words end abruptly when I go completely stiff, and she shakes her head and tries to backtrack, but it's too late. I get it. "I mean—"

"It's fine, Kylee," I say and try not to feel so gutted. "I know I'm not the kind of guy a girl brings home to Daddy."

"Jamie, I didn't mean that."

"Have you decided to help?" Jace asks when he comes back into the room.

"You want the food edible?" I say, working to keep a lightness in my tone, even though there's a shit storm going on inside me.

He shoos me away, like Gram always does. "Then get out."

I go back to the family room, plunk down into my chair, and watch the game for the next few hours, a restless energy building inside me. I'm not used to sitting idle for so long. As Kylee pops into the room every once in a while to check on the score, I try not to feel pissed off. I mean come on. Boundaries were set when we started this thing. Did I really think she'd want to bring me home to Daddy? Fuck no. I don't want that anyway.

Yeah, keep telling yourself that, dude.

Summer and Sean eventually wake from their nap and join us, but baby Devon remains sleeping in his crib upstairs. When Gram finally gets up and makes her way downstairs, everyone is called to the table.

Once again we're all seated around the room, and Kylee is next to Jared. How the little prick manages that every time is beyond me. But I don't want to start showing too much interest and give everyone the wrong idea—like I'm batshit crazy about her or something.

Kylee seems much more comfortable around the table this time, and when Tyler starts razzing Jared about something she turns to Gram.

"How did you do it with all boys?"

She laughs. "They were a handful, that's for sure. But they're all sweet boys."

Kylee looks at me and grins, and I wonder if her mind is traveling the same road as mine—when I showed her just how *not* sweet I really was.

"I bet you have a lot of stories," Kylee says, then slides her fork into her mouth. I try not to watch the way her lips part, try not to think about how my dick felt in her mouth. But I'd have more luck trying to levitate the house with my mind. I am so fucked.

"Oh, I have lots of stories."

Groans come from around the table, and Summer laughs. "Let's just say every guy at this table could be the poster boy for authority issues. They listened to Gram though."

"Oh?" she says.

Gram eyes each boy. "If they didn't I'd gristle them."

"Gristle?"

"It's just a term Gram uses, but it's effective," Summer explains. "Just the thought of getting gristled sent these big tough guys into hysterics."

"No one wanted to get gristled," Sean says. He shakes. "Gram has the boniest knuckles."

Since I'm the closest to her, Gram reaches out to me, and I flinch. "Hey, I'm just sitting here minding my own business."

She grabs my side and pinches, then rubs her knuckles against my rib cage. I go weak in the knees, become boneless as she "gristles" me. We all laugh and Kylee's voice stands out the most to me. I love the sound, maybe even more than the noises she makes when she's coming for me.

"So you can see why no one wanted to get gristled, right?" Summer says.

"I'll have to remember that move when I have kids," Kylee says, and as soon as the words leave her mouth, her smile falls and her gaze darts to mine. Our eyes meet, collide, hold for a moment too long.

"So you're thinking about having kids now, are you?" Gram says, clearly not letting that one go.

"No, I just meant . . . I, ah . . ."

"Kylee has a career to think about right now, Gram. Her statement was hypothetical," I say, coming to her rescue, and she gives me a grateful smile. Conversation gets turned to baby Devon and which one of us guys will be the godfather. Everyone but me is fighting for the right. I have no idea about kids and wouldn't want to fuck the kid up. Summer will have to pick outside the family for the godmother, since she's the only girl in the family—so far. And it doesn't look like any of us are about to change that any time soon. I know I'm not.

When the meal is done, I give Gram a kiss and excuse myself. I need to get to the shop and get some more work done. I've been so busy with Kylee, if I don't get to the shop, I'll never get it open in time.

"I'll stop by and get Scout on my way home," I say to Kylee.

"Okay, see you at home," she says.

My gut twists at the word *home*. Is that what I want? To make a home with sweet Kylee Jensen? Fuck, I've been down this road, have the scars to prove it.

I say my goodbyes to everyone and make my way outside. The cooler night air is welcome against my heated skin. I jump into my truck and drive to my shop, my thoughts calming when I walk inside my sanctuary. I flick the lights on, glance around, then put drop cloths over the furniture. Tonight I think I'll paint. I find it relaxing, and maybe it will help me clear my thoughts and get my head back on straight where Kylee is concerned. I jack the tunes and pour the paint over into the tray. I dip the roller in and start on the wall, but stop when I hear my door open.

I turn, and the second I see sweet Kylee walking in, my heart jumps into my throat and pretty much does the fucking Macarena. Yeah, I guess I kinda do want it all with her—and that's never going to happen.

"Hi," I say, my stomach still twisted up in knots from our earlier conversation. I hated the look on Jamie's face, the tension in his posture, when I jumped all over his question about my father. I sure let him know, in no uncertain terms, that I'd never tell my father about us. I'd hurt him with that thoughtless outburst, and really, it was more what I didn't say than what I did that hurt him the most—my father would never accept a man like him into our family. I spent my whole life pleasing my father, following his orders, but when it comes right down to it, I don't want to be like him and refuse to judge someone based on their lot in life. From the scars on Jamie's body to the demons in his eyes, I know he's been cut deeply. But underneath it all, he's a good man. The best man I know.

"Hey," he says, but the light in his eyes is a bit dimmer tonight.

I close the door and step up to him. I put my hand on his chest, feel his racing heart. "Jamie, about earlier. My father—"

He shakes his head, and his big, warm hand closes over mine. "It's fine, Kylee," he says. "I know your father is controlling, and you don't have to worry. He'll never know about us."

I open my mouth to say more, but what can I say? We both clearly want to keep our affair a secret, for our own personal reasons—his I still don't know—but that doesn't change the fact that I feel a little hollowed-out inside, or that I might want so much more from a man not willing to give it. How could we possibly make a life together anyway? My father aside, Jamie lives here in Blue Bay with secrets he keeps close, and my life, and a future my father is pushing down my throat, is waiting for me in Atlanta. I pinch my lips shut and look at the roller in his hand.

"Want some help?"

He steps back, gazes the length of me. "You're hardly dressed for painting."

I take in his T-shirt and jeans. "Neither are you, really. You could ruin your clothes just as well as I could."

"It doesn't matter if I get paint on these old things, but you're in a dress, one you made. It has value, and I'd hate myself if you ruined it after all the hard work you put into making it."

My heart thumps at his sweetness. "Well then, I guess there's only one way to rectify that."

"What might that be?"

"I could paint naked."

A huge smile spreads across his face, and in that instant, I relax. I might have hurt him earlier tonight, but I know we're going to be okay, at least for the rest of the summer. When I leave, however . . .

"Really?"

"Sure." I reach for the hem of my dress, and rub the material through my fingers. "If you'll get naked too."

He pinches the bridge of his nose. "Kylee, if we get naked, I'll never get this painting done."

"Sure we will. Painting is boring, and this will help liven it up, don't you think?"

"Oh I think it's going to liven *it* up all right. And by *it*, I mean my cock."

I laugh, and the sweetest, softest smile tugs at his mouth as he angles his head and watches me, like he loves the sounds I'm making.

"Deal?" I ask and hold my hand out to his for a shake.

He takes my hand in his and his warmth seeps under my skin. "You really want to help?"

"I do."

"Okay." He steps up to the windows and draws the blinds. "But I don't want anyone but me looking at your body."

His protectiveness warms my heart. "Sweet boy."

He winks at me and bumps the temperature, another caring, protective gesture. "Sweet boy? Haven't we been over that?"

"Strip," I say, and point a finger at him.

We both take our clothes off, and I admire his body as he sheds his pants and top in record time. We drape our things over the tattoo chair and Jamie covers it with a cloth to keep our clothes from getting destroyed. He's pretty damn erect when he turns back to me, and I can't take my eyes off his cock.

I try to appear unaffected, bored even, despite the fact that the needy juncture between my legs is begging me to jump him. "You'd better rein that in," I say and gesture with a nod toward his erection. "Otherwise it could get in the way."

A deep, tortured sound catches in his throat. "Like I have any control over my dick when the most beautiful girl in the world is standing before me completely naked." He scrubs his chin and looks like he's in total agony. "Believe me, little Jamie is not going down anytime soon."

He thinks I'm the most beautiful girl in the world?

"Little Jamie is not so little right now," I say and tap my chin, like I'm deep in thought, even though my brain is buzzing and my body is practically convulsing with need. "Maybe we could put him to use."

Heat moves into his eyes as his gaze roams my body. My nipples tighten under his hot, appreciative stare. "Yeah?" he asks as his cock grows another inch. "I know plenty of ways we could do that."

"What I'm thinking is, we stick a roller on the end. Double your efforts, and get this done twice as fast."

He glares at me, but I see the humor in the depths of his gorgeous green eyes. "The only thing I want on the end of my cock is your smart-ass mouth."

"That can be arranged," I say and take in the desire reflecting in his eyes. "After we paint. This is important to you, so it's important to me too."

He looks at me like he wants to say something, and I can only hope the words that come out of his mouth next are, "You're important to me." Instead he hands me a roller and points to the wall behind him.

"Maybe you should start on that wall, where I can't see you."

"No, I want to see you." I dip my roller into the paint, and walk up to the wall he'd been working on. "This is a nice shade of gray. I like it."

"Thanks," he says, his voice tight, his muscles clenching as he steps to the other end of the wall, away from me. I grin, secretly liking that I can do this to him.

When an old song comes on the radio, I begin to hum. After a minute I look at Jamie, see the way he's staring at me. "What?" I ask.

"You're humming," he says through gritted teeth. "This is enough torture as it is, and you know what your humming does to me."

"Oh," I say. "Oops, sorry." I reload my roller and continue painting. We work in silence for a while, and I consider Jamie's chosen profession. What is it about ink that he loves so much?

"Why tattooing?" I ask, breaking the quiet. I glance at Jamie, who is studying me too closely, too intensely. My fingers tighten on the roller handle. How long has he been watching me?

"Truthfully?" he asks, a new seriousness about him.

"Yes," I say, wanting him to open up, tell me more about himself.

"I've always loved drawing." He runs the roller along the wall, then stands back to examine his progress. "I used to drive my teachers crazy with all the doodling I did in class." A smile curls up the corners of his mouth, like the memory takes him back to a happy place. "I thought I'd be a cartoonist or a famous painter when I grew up." He goes quiet for a moment, then angles his head to see me. "I've never told anyone that before. I never wanted it to get back to my father, I guess. He was hard enough on me for being a dreamer."

"There's nothing wrong with being a dreamer, Jamie."

He shrugs. "Dreams don't pay the bills." He shakes his head. "That's what Dad used to say."

"I know all about that."

He nods. "I know you do." He reloads his roller and starts to paint again, and I wait patiently for him to continue with his story. "When I was about twelve, my mom took me to the orthodontist in Hope Falls." He flashes perfect white teeth in a smile. "Braces. Anyway, we walked by this tattoo shop, and I was fascinated by the art displayed in the windows. Right then and there I knew what I wanted to do."

"You're very brave, Jamie."

His head rears back. "Brave? How am I brave?"

I shrug and reload my roller. "You found your passion and didn't let anyone or anything deter you from pursuing it." Sadness moves into his eyes as he looks at me. "Your artwork is beautiful. You have a rare talent, and I'm so glad you're doing something with it," I say.

"See, it's more than just artwork to me. It's a way of expressing myself, a way for others to express themselves." He stops painting and grabs his sketchbook. "These designs, they all mean something to me." The passion in his voice, his childlike enthusiasm as he explains his art, wrap around my heart and squeeze. I love seeing him like this.

He sits in a chair and opens the book on his lap. "I can't even explain what it does to me when someone comes into my shop and asks me to design something special for them, something that has a deeper meaning. They put that kind of trust in me."

I set my roller beside his, grab one of the vinyl chairs, and set it across from him. I sit and our knees bump. "Can I see?"

"Sure." He turns the book on his lap and as I look at the designs, he continues. "People get tattoos for lots of reasons, and when I can give them ink that holds a deeper meaning, and it touches them on another level, well...I can't even explain what that does to me." He exhales and shakes his head as he runs his hands through his hair.

I swallow and practically vibrate as I absorb his passionate energy. "These are so beautiful, Jamie," I say and flip through the pages. "If your father could have seen these, seen how passionate you are about your work, I think he would have been so proud of you. I'm sad that he didn't understand this side of you."

He shrugs, but I see the pain etched on his face. With exquisite gentleness, he brushes my hair from my shoulders, exposing my naked breasts. "If you were to ever get one, what would you like?" he asks.

I shake my head. "I have no idea. What do most girls get?"

"Everyone gets something different." He runs his hand along my arm, and I look at him, unable to believe I'm having this deep, meaningful conversation with Jamie as we paint his shop bare naked. Did life get any better than this?

I close the book on my lap, and he sets it on the counter beside him. "If you were to design one for me, what would it be?"

"That's easy. I'd give you the Viking symbol." His hand slides between my legs and spreads them. "Right here, where it could be our little secret."

"What's the Viking symbol?" He reaches for his pen, and draws two Vs on his hand, one on top of the other. "What does it mean?" I ask as I trace it with my finger.

He cups my chin. "It means create your own reality." I look down and think about that. I'm not brave like Jamie. I never stood up to my father and instead let him pull my strings and lead me around like I was a marionette and he was the puppet master. It generates a deep sadness inside me.

"Kylee," Jamie says, his voice softer, lower.

"Yeah."

"I know it's not my business, but the clothes you design are beautiful and have value."

I swallow. There is nothing mocking in his tone—like I'm used to from my father—and it's oddly sweet how he shows such interest in my designs.

"I just . . . I know you'll be a great lawyer, but I hate to see you stifle your passion. I see how happy you are when you're creating, and your clothes would sell like this." He snaps his fingers and my heart wobbles, his compliment meaning more to me than he'd ever know.

"Thank you," I say and lean into him. His lips caress mine, and he pulls me onto his lap. We sit together, completely naked, like we've done this a million times before. It's a bit insane how quickly we've grown so comfortable with each other.

"I need to tell you something, and I don't want you to get upset."

I go still. Am I finally going to find out why he wants to keep us a secret? "Okay," I say.

"I went in to Indigo Blue Boutique today."

I crinkle my nose. "Why? You don't strike me as the kind of guy to walk into a specialty store like that. They sell high-end clothes and stock lots of lingerie."

"Yeah, no kidding," he says, and scrubs his chin, like the incident will haunt him forever. "But I wanted to talk to the manager." I go quiet, my heart thumping a little louder as understanding dawns. "She takes clothes on consignment. I thought—"

"You thought I could put some of my designs in her shop."

"You've been making so much, you have a huge inventory."

Little did he know what I was doing with those clothes, though. "You shouldn't have done that, Jamie," I say, even though I'm completely touched by the gesture. My whole life my father made decisions for me. Now Jamie thinks he can dictate where I should sell my clothes. But he's doing it for a whole other reason, and I'm deeply moved by the gesture. In fact, I feel an unfamiliar fullness in my chest, right around the vicinity of my heart.

"I know. I overstepped boundaries." He takes my hand and kisses my fingers, one at a time. "Are you mad?"

"Yeah, I'm mad," I say, but I'm not. How could I stay mad at a man who shows such interest in my hobby?

"Maybe I can make it up to you." He runs his hands along my shoulders, and shivery goose bumps form in their wake.

"Just how do you plan to do that?" I ask as sexual energy arcs between us.

His dirty, sexy grin returns. "I could put my cock inside you."

"I thought you needed to get the painting done," I say, my body aching for him to do just that and more.

He moves his hips and his hard cock presses against the seam along my ass. I bite my lip to keep myself from groaning. "I've had the hard-on of the century for the last half hour. I'm sure this will be quick."

I squirm on his lap and throw one leg around his until I'm straddling his thighs, his long hard length now pressing against my sex. I wiggle, and the pressure on my clit is so deliciously delightful I nearly come. He lifts me, and I reach between us to position his hard cock at my entrance. He lowers me onto him, and I expel a heavy breath as he enters me. I love the way he feels inside me. How the hell am I ever going to go on after I leave this place—leave this man?

"You feel so good," he murmurs and takes one of my nipples into his mouth. His hands span my waist and he lifts me up and down effortlessly. I'm so wet his cock slides in and out easily, and my breathing changes, becomes harsher.

"So good," I agree, and arch into him as he nibbles on my pebbled nub. I run my hands through his hair as he rocks into me, his groans curling around me and seeping under my skin. We move together, our bodies so in tune with each other. A storm builds inside me as I ride him and with deep, explicit strokes that take me to amazing places, I moan softly against his ear. He groans, and I grip the top of the chair behind him and gyrate on his cock, taking him deeper inside my body, wanting to keep him there forever.

"Jamie," I whisper.

"Yeah."

"I want a tattoo. I want to be your first client when we get this place open."

"We?"

"Yes, I want to help you. I have some ideas." I inch back to see him. "Unless you don't want my help"

"Of course I want your help." His fingers bite into my skin. "But I have to tell you. There is no blood left in my brain, so I'd pretty much agree to anything right now."

"Well then, how about you—" I begin but he cups the back of my neck and brings my mouth to his.

"I don't have to be lust-drunk to give you what you want, Kylee. Ask me for anything, and it's yours."

My heart takes a tumble. *Anything.* Oh, if he only knew what was rattling around inside my brain, how much I want to ask for his heart. Honest to God, the plan was to have an affair with the hot carpenter and for once in my life do something just for me. Little did I think I'd fall for him, and his family, and even the damn dog. But I did, and that was just stupid of me.

"You okay?" he asks, and runs his lips over my neck.

I really love the way he always checks in with me. "Yeah, why?" I fib, sure I'm never going to be okay again.

"You went quiet. Were you thinking about what you might want to ask me for?" he queries as he moves his hips and powers into me. I rake my nails over his flesh, drag skin, as heat flares through me. I'm so close but I don't want to come just yet. I want more, everything, from this man.

"Yes. I want you to take me, Jamie. Everywhere, like you talked about."

He goes still, and his eyes meet mine. "Yeah?"

"Yes," I say. "I need to feel you inside me. Everywhere."

"I need that too," he says and his hands move urgently over my body. "But I would never do anything to your body you're not ready for. You put your trust in my hands, and that's not something I take lightly. I'm not saying I won't do it, it just won't be tonight, here at the shop." He kisses my throat and his breath whispers over my body. "I want you home in your bed, where you'll be completely comfortable."

My heart nearly explodes in my chest, and tears prick my eyes as I tremble with all the things I feel for him.

He slides his fingers between my legs, and the second he brushes my clit I come all over him. I rock my hips and ride out the waves as they continue to crash over me, each one harder than the last, until I'm a quivering mess on his lap.

"Jamie," I murmur and press my lips to his.

"Fuck, you're so beautiful, Kylee," he says as I drip over his cock. He holds me tighter and releases inside me. His deep growl curls around me and brings a smile to my face. I love reducing this big bad tattoo artist to a hot mess.

We hold each other for a long time, then he cups my shoulders and inches back to see me. His gaze moves over my face, and he cups my cheek. "You good?" he asks.

"I am," I say my heart ready to rupture. "You?"

He nods. "You know . . ." he begins.

"Know what?"

"If you're going to help me paint this place, I'm going to need you in a big-ass pair of coveralls."

I laugh and he chuckles with me. "I'll pick us each up a pair tomorrow," I say.

"Then again," he murmurs, as his lips close over mine, "I still don't think that's going to stop me from wanting to ravage you."

13

JAMIE

The last two weeks flew by in a blur. I finally finished the deck, Summer and Sean are back in their cottage with their new baby, and I've moved on to helping Ryan with another roofing project. Even though I'm no longer working on Kylee's place, it hasn't kept me away from her. We've fallen into a routine of working on the shop to get it up and ready, watching all these old movies she loves, slipping into bed together every night, and more importantly, waking up in each other's arms every morning. We've gone from calling each other *boy* and *girl* in bed to *Jamie* and *Kylee*, and when she uses my name and I use hers, it's easy to forget we're playing roles.

Also over the last two weeks, tourists have begun trickling in, and thankfully, I've not seen any more activity at the Jacki-noff cottage. Kylee, however, is still receiving phone calls from her dad, and on days when she's not in her spare bedroom making clothes or on the beach sketching in her book, she sometimes disappears for hours. I still have no idea where she goes, and she's still not supplying the information.

Even though we've grown closer, closer than I have to any other woman, I guess we still have secrets.

I take off my ball cap and run my hand over my hair after a hot day on the roof. I pull open the back screen door to Kylee's cottage and when I find her in the kitchen humming as she tosses together a salad, my cock thickens.

"How was your day?" I ask and lean against the doorjamb, just wanting to watch her.

She turns, and her smile widens when she sees me. "It was good. I got a lot of work done, oh, and look at these." She dries her hands on the tea towel and hold up her sketchbook. I love when she's happy like this.

"You have been busy," I say, loving the normalcy in our routine, maybe a little too much.

"How was your day? Did the last of your equipment arrive for the shop?"

I nod. "Yeah, we should be able to meet our grand opening deadline next Monday."

She claps her hands together and squeals, and my heart flips. The way she supports me and is so happy to see me finally get my shop up and running is a total mind fuck.

"Need help with that?" I ask and point to the salad.

She frowns. "Did you forget we're going to Summer and Sean's for the barbecue tonight?"

"Uh, yeah, I guess I did. Actually I didn't know they asked you. I thought they were just having the guys over."

"Apparently not. Summer called me last week. She told me Sean asked you."

Unease moves through me. Does Sean know what I'm up to with Kylee? Is he inviting all the guys over or just me to remind me of past mistakes? He knows how it turned out for me last time and why I now have my motto: Don't get involved with pampered girls who spend their summers in Blue Bay. Or is Summer up to something else? I know how she and Gram are always butting into our business and trying to get all the guys hitched.

"Do they know about us?" I ask Kylee.

"Jamie, I've not said anything but your truck is parked in my driveway every night. How could they not?"

"Shit, you're right," I say under my breath, and Kylee glances down, averting her eyes. Fuck, now I've hurt her feelings. "It's not . . . I just. I don't want anyone getting the wrong idea."

That I might love her. That she might destroy me.

"I know," she says quietly, then lifts her head, her smile forced. "You'd better get showered, we're supposed to be there in ten minutes. Oh, and Gram stopped by today."

"Yeah, why?"

"Last time I was at Sunday dinner, we started talking about you guys as kids. She told me she had a special photo album for each of you guys."

"Oh, yeah? I didn't know that."

"Anyway, she brought it over. I haven't looked though it yet. I wanted to do it with you."

"Because you need me present when you laugh at all the stupid things I've done?"

"Of course," she says breezily, her lips quirking. "It's no fun laughing at you if you're not here to see me do it."

I cross the room, step up to her, and drop a kiss onto her mouth, but then something else occurs to me. I push her hair from her face and her look is warm, dreamy as she gazes up at me.

"So I guess Gram knows where I've been spending my nights, too. Otherwise she wouldn't have brought my album."

She nods. "I think everyone in town knows, Jamie."

"I guess it's a good thing your dad is in Atlanta then, huh?"

"Yeah," she says quietly, and frowns, like the mention of her father has triggered an unpleasant memory.

Wanting to see her smile again, I say, "Okay, give me five minutes to shower." I tug off my sweaty T-shirt and her hot gaze races over me. "Or maybe we could take ten minutes and you could join me."

"If I join you, we'll never get to Summer's, and I don't want to be late the first time she invites me to dinner." She points to the hall. "Go and I'll stay here and try not to think about how hot you look without a shirt on."

I hurry to the shower and hope it wasn't just me and Kylee invited to the barbecue. I'm so not in a mood to get lectured by my big brother. I rinse off quickly, grab clean jeans and T-shirt from the basket of laundry Kylee did, and meet her in the kitchen.

"All set?" she asks, having changed from her shorts to a sexy summer dress that hugs her curves and teases my cock.

"You look hot," I say. "You sure you don't just want to stay here and let me get you out of that dress?"

"No, I'm not sure, I would love nothing more than to get naked with you, but I don't want to leave Summer hanging either, so let's go." She scoops up the salad and I follow her out. We head a few doors down, and when I reach Sean's place and realize we're the only ones who've been invited, I get a lump in my throat.

"Hey bro," I say and step up to Sean as he tosses steaks onto the grill. "Need any help?"

"Hey, you two." He turns to Kylee. "Summer is inside changing the baby. Just go on in. She's expecting you." He looks back at me. "You're not getting near this grill. Just grab us a couple beers."

"Why does nobody think I can cook?" I ask

Kylee hovers at the door and listens for a second. "Are you forgetting the time you nearly set the house on fire when you decided to roast a marshmallow over a candle?" Sean asks.

"I was nine," I say. "I've been living on my own for a long time now. I can cook. I just don't like to."

"I'll believe it when I see it," he says laughing.

I follow Kylee inside and take the salad from her. I place it in the fridge and grab two beers. Kylee makes her way to the sofa, where Summer is just finishing with Devon. Scout jumps from her bed, her tail wagging madly when she sees Kylee coming her way.

Yeah, I get it girl. My tail wags when I see Kylee coming too.

"I'm so glad you two could come," Summer says. "I need the adult company."

Kylee smiles. "Have you been getting any sleep?"

"Not a whole lot."

I leave the girls to talk and step back outside. I twist the caps off the beers and hand one to my brother. He closes the grill and we both plop down into the Adirondack chairs he built.

"How's the roof coming?" he asks, starting with the small talk, but soon enough he'll get to the real question, like what the fuck do I think I'm doing with Kylee.

"Good, no problems at all."

"How's the shop?"

"We're going to make our opening deadline." I hold my beer up and he clicks his bottle with mine.

"We're?"

"Yeah." I gesture with a nod behind me. "Kylee has been helping me."

He opens his mouth like he wants to say something but Summer and Kylee, with Devon in her arms, along with Scout, make an appearance.

"How long for the steaks?" Summer asks as she drops a kiss onto her husband's mouth. "I'm starving."

"A few more minutes."

Kylee turns to me. "Want to hold your nephew?"

"I . . . Jesus . . ."

"No swearing around the baby," Sean says, and that warning coming from the man with the foulest mouth of us all leaves me shaking my head. Having a family has changed him so much—for the better.

"Here, don't be afraid," Kylee says.

I crook my arms for her to place Devon into them. I hold my little nephew, and his fingers wrap around my thumb. "Hey little dude," I say. "I'm your uncle Jamie, and you and me, well, I'm going to teach you all kinds of things."

"Over my dead body," Sean says, grinning.

"Don't worry. We can have our own secrets," I say and wink at him. He smiles back. "Shit . . . I mean, ah, did you guys see that?" This no-swearing thing is going to take some effort.

"See what?" Summer asks.

"He smiled at me."

"It's gas, Jamie," Sean explains.

I angle my head, look over the cute bald dude in my arms. My heart pinches a bit as I fall hopelessly in love with him. "Ignore him," I say to Devon. "The two of us, we're going to get in all kinds of trouble together." I glance up and when I see how still Kylee has become, the way her eyes are saucer-big as I rock Devon in my arms, I ask, "Want to hold him?"

"Sure." She sits next to me, and I hand him over. She brings him to her shoulder like a natural and rocks him. In no time at all, heavy lashes fall over green eyes and he goes to sleep.

"That's the life," I say. "Rocked to sleep by a pretty girl."

Summer stands to take the baby from Kylee. "Here, let me put him to bed, and then we can eat."

A few minutes later we're all seated at the picnic table, and the sun dips lower in the sky. The sounds of children on the beach fade as they head back home after a busy day, and waves crash gently on the shore. I kick back and enjoy the meal my brother and sister-in-law prepared for us.

"How are you enjoying Blue Bay?" Summer asks Kylee.

She frowns. "I love it here."

"Why the frown?" Summer asks.

"I guess because I'm not looking forward to leaving at the end of the summer." Her glance flickers to mine, and my heart thuds. Is it possible she wants to stay—with me? Do I dare hope? She shrugs and tosses her hands up in the air. "But I have to get back to reality sooner or later, right?"

I want to tell her, *reality is overrated,* but I don't. I also quickly squelch the hope rising up in me and dig into my steak.

For the rest of the meal, we talk about work, the baby, and my shop, keeping the conversation light and easy. By the time we clear the dishes and grab another beer, the girls go inside to tend to Devon and I walk back outside with Sean. When the hell is he going to start lecturing me? The wait is killer.

"Come on," he says and we move further down the beach, away from the house, where our conversation can be private. Sean drops to the warm sand, and I follow him down. We lay on our backs and stare up at the stars, like we did so many times in our youth. Just Sean and me. Best buds. Back then I never kept secrets from him.

"How long have you loved her?" he finally asks, breaking the quiet around us.

I roll to my side and prop up on my elbow. "Who says I love her?"

"Give me a fucking break, Jamie. I know you better than anyone."

I exhale slowly, and Sean turns toward me, mimicking my positions.

"That obvious, huh?"

He nods. "Yeah."

"Why did you put me on her deck job?"

"Summer thought I should. I wasn't sure at first, but I trust that my wife knows what she's doing."

I fall back and stare at the sky. "She's a rich girl looking for fun. I tried to keep my distance, Sean. I really did. But I'm fucking weak."

"You're not weak, Jamie. You're one of the toughest fucking guys I know. Christ, you just about took down four guys on your own."

I think back to the day the Jackinoff boys beat the crap out of me. "I should have walked away from Kylee."

"And now you can't."

"No, but soon enough she'll be walking away from me and Blue Bay."

"If you love her so much, why don't you give her a reason to stay?"

I angle my head to see my brother, the smartest guy I know, who I love with all my heart. "What's here for her, Sean?"

Green eyes lock on mine. "You."

We both go quiet for a long time as I mull that over. "I can't ask her to give up her career, something she's worked so hard for."

"There's work here for her and there are big law firms in Hope Falls."

Hope Falls. That's where she's been going when she disappears for hours. I only know because she always has a fresh Starbucks coffee cup in her car cup holder when she returns. What the hell could she be doing in Hope Falls? Maybe she is thinking about staying and is there looking for work. Or maybe I'm just grasping at straws.

"Who says it's even what she wants?" I ask.

"I do," Sean replies. "I see the way you two look at each other." A pause and then, "Or she could hang her own shingle here on the beach, like Summer did. Then again, from the way she talks about law, it sounds like she hates it."

"I know." My mind races back to Indigo Blue Boutique. She could definitely find work there, or better yet . . . "I'm pretty sure her father would disown her if she stayed here. He's a controlling prick."

Sean scoffs. "When have you ever been afraid of a controlling prick?"

"Never."

"That's what I thought."

"So what are you saying, Sean? You think this thing between me and Kylee—"

"Has you all fucked up, and you need to do something before it's too late."

"What the hell am I supposed to do?"

"You're a smart guy and know her better than I do. Figure it out."

I sit up and finish my beer. "We'd better get back."

Sean climbs to his feet and we make our way back to the cottage. Summer is pretty tired out, and I reach for Kylee, and since these two know all about us, I pull her into my arms, unable to take another second without feeling her beside me. At first she seems surprised by my public display of affection, then she softens against me.

I nod toward the door. "We should get going, let these two get some sleep."

"Okay," she says quietly and we say our goodbyes. We walk along the beach on our way back to Kylee's place, and once we're inside, we settle ourselves on the sofa.

I yawn, but Kylee jabs me. "Hey, don't go to sleep on me. I've been dying to look at your photo album."

I moan. "Do we have to? Wouldn't you rather get naked and let me slide into you?" Her body quivers and her lids go heavy.

"I want that, but first pictures."

"Fine, if you're going to look at my kid photos, I want to see yours."

"You'll have to come to Atlanta. I don't have any here."

Reality hits as soon as she brings up Atlanta. Would I travel to Atlanta and make a life there if that's what she wanted? Yeah, I fucking would. But who says that's what she wants.

She peels open the album and laughs when she sees my kindergarten picture. "Oh, my God, Jamie. You were so cute."

"Were?" I ask and pull her closer, until her warm body is meshed next to mine.

"Now you're handsome," she says, her gaze moving over my face, lingering over the scar on my jaw.

She flips the pages, and I sit up a little straighter, surprised to see my photos through the years, everything from kindergarten right up until high school. The last photo in the book is my high school graduation, probably because I skipped town shortly after. I'm a little touched that Gram put this book together for me. I don't remember being photographed much as a kid.

After going through every single picture and wanting me to tell a story of what I was doing in each one, Kylee yawns and closes the book, but a loose picture falls out.

"Oops," she says and reaches for it. She examines it, and then narrows her eyes. "Jamie . . ." she turns to me, her mouth agape, her eyes wide open. "Is this . . . ?"

I take the picture from her and my heart goes into my throat. I stare, unable to speak or even breathe. Ice freezes my blood and I gulp air as chaos erupts inside me. Tears prick my eyes, and I fight them back as loss overcomes me, rattles me to my very core. Grief hits like a punch to the gut, and for a moment I let it wrap around me like a deadly snake and suck the oxygen from my lungs. I want to drop to the floor and curl up in it, let it consume me, eat me alive, but the hand on my face pulls me back.

"Jamie?" Kylee says.

"It's . . . Dad," I say and look at the picture again. I could never do right in the man's eyes, had disappointed him so much when I left town. How long had he waited for me—all of us—to come back? We all eventually returned to Blue Bay, but it was too late to fix past mistakes. Was this Dad's way of mending bridges, of showing me his support, that he might have actually understood my passion and been proud of what I was doing? Tears are falling down Kylee's face when I look at her, and my wobbly heart squeezes.

"Jamie," she whispers and cups my face.

Before Kylee, I'd never let anyone see my pain, my tears. But Kylee isn't just anyone. I'm in love with her, and in my heart, I know what we have is the real deal. "I had no idea."

She sniffs and says, "He was proud of you, Jamie."

I take a shuddery breath and look at the two four-leaf clover tattoos on my father's back, the names of his five sons and three nephews etched on each leaf. A big hiccupping sob catches in my throat and I briefly pinch my eyes shut. This was no small thing he did, and deep in my heart I know he did it for me. The clovers aren't random, they're a sign of luck, have a special meaning, and were chosen very carefully by my father. What this tells me is he understood what it was I did, and why I did it.

"I never thought in a million years he'd get a tattoo." I pull Kylee to me and press a kiss onto her mouth. My heart pounds hard against my chest, my thoughts on a roller coaster ride. I feel like I'm dying, yet so alive at the same time. One thing I do know for certain is I need to be inside Kylee again.

I *have* to.

14

JAMIE

"Are we ready for this?" I ask and glance around my new shop, taking in the excited faces of my entire family: Gram, Sean, Tyler, Ryan, Jace, Jared, Carter, Jacob, Summer, baby Devon . . . and Kylee.

Technically Kylee isn't family, but still, I couldn't have done this, or gotten it ready by my deadline, if it weren't for her help and ideas.

My heart goes into my throat when I see her big smile. "Let's do this," she says, and gestures toward the door to the group of eager people waiting outside. As I make my way toward the door to invite everyone in for coffee and cake, compliments of Gram, Kylee releases the balloons into the shop.

Her idea was to have customers pop the balloons and win specials. She spent hours writing out discount cards, stuffing them into the balloons, and blowing them up.

I open the door and the noise level in my small shop jumps as excited patrons all file in to help celebrate. Balloons are popped and I'm soon lost in the excitement.

Gram and the guys all greet my new clientele—show them

my sketches—and I'm surprised to see a few familiar faces from the summer vacationers. That thought has my mind once again going back to the Jackinoffs, but I push it away. Today is my day, something I've been working toward for a long time, and I'm not going to let anything or anyone bring me down. I catch Kylee's gaze from across the room as she chats with people and makes appointments for me.

I work the room myself and eventually make my way to the counter. My heart fills with emotions when I take in the corkboard beside the cash register. The first thing I did after finding that picture of Dad was bring it here and hang it. I know he's not here to see me open my own shop, but he's here in spirit, and to know he was proud of me, well . . . My throat clogs with emotion, and I work to swallow it down as Gram steps up to me.

She touches my cheek, and as if knowing where my thoughts were, she says, "Your father would have been so proud of you, sweet boy."

"Thanks Gram," I say and wrap my arms around her. I don't care who's watching. I pick her up and spin her and she lets out a yelp that has a few people laughing.

An hour or so later the crowd dies down, and the guys help Gram clear away the leftover cake. Soon enough it's just Kylee and me and a room full of scattered balloons.

"Jesus," I say and rake my hand through my hair.

Kylee laughs. "That's all you have to say?"

"I guess I'm just a little overwhelmed."

"Well you should be. Look at this." She grabs my reservation book and shows me all the appointments. "You're going to be busy for months, Jamie." She goes up on her toes and plants a soft kiss onto my mouth. "I'm so proud of you. You followed your dreams, and you made this happen."

"Kylee, I want this for you," I say.

She presses her fingers to my lips. "Today is about you," she says.

My heart pinches, because there are so many other dreams I have, other things I want to happen, but how do I go about telling her how I feel, what I want. What if I tell her and she runs back to Atlanta? What if she doesn't?

Guess there is only one way to find out, because Sean is right, she does have me all fucked up and I need to figure out what to do about it. An idea forms, takes shape in my mind, and while I'm eager to get started, to show her once and for all how I feel, what I want, first things first.

I scoop her up and she squeals when I set her on my tattoo chair. "All night, I've been thinking about this," I say and plant my mouth on hers.

I kiss her long and deep, and she returns it readily, always so open and ready for me that it totally fucks with my mind and body.

"Oh, really," she says as my mouth moves to her breasts.

"Yeah, really," I murmur as I peel her blouse open and press my lips to her nipples, licking her through her lace bra.

Her hands slide around my head, hold me to her, and she moans as I nip at her hard buds.

"Want to know what I've been thinking?"

"Always," I say.

Her hand slides down my body, and she captures my hard cock. "How about I show you instead."

15

KYLEE

As the end of July approaches and all the vacationers are back in town, I've seen less and less of Jamie. I know his workload has doubled with people wanting renovations or repairs to their cottages, and he's opened his shop, so in the evenings he's busy with his clientele, plus he's teaching Ryan the art of tattooing. Every time I talk about stopping in to the shop to see him, he makes an excuse and tells me not to come. I can't help but wonder if he's pulling back because soon enough I'll be leaving here, and it's his way of reminding me this relationship is sex and sex only.

Was I so foolish to think it might have been more, that what we've been doing is making love to each other every night, and that his passionate, soft kisses come from his heart and not a place farther south? Even if he did want more, like I do, how could it work out between us? When I start practicing law, I'll be working eighteen-hour days. If that leaves no room for a family, how could I possibly think I could pull off a long-distance relationship?

I'm not sure, but there is a part of me that can't let this

go. In my heart, this thing between Jamie and me is real, and I'd be a fool to turn my back on a once-in-a-lifetime love. A sense of urgency races through me. I need to talk to Jamie, to see if he feels the same way, and I need to do it now.

I reach for my car keys, ready to hunt him down, when a knock comes at my front door. I rush to it, hoping it's Jamie yet knowing in my heart it's not. He has his own key and always comes in the screen door at the back of the house. I pull the door open and when I come face to face with my father and Trevor Jackson, my heart falls into my stomach and I go still, perfectly motionless.

"Now, is that any way to treat your father," my dad says as I stand there, shell-shocked.

I blink, sure I'm hallucinating, but when I open my eyes again, my father is still standing there. "What, how . . . ?"

My father, overbearing man that he is, pushes past me and walks into my place like he owns it. The place was a graduation gift to me, bought with his money, but that doesn't mean it's his, right?

"Trevor's family were all gathering for a reunion at their cottage, just a few doors down from here, and I decided to tag along, see what has my daughter so busy that she can't make time to take her father's calls." He moves to the back of the house, and I turn to Trevor, who is smiling down at me, a grin on his mouth like he knows exactly why I haven't been taking my father's calls. But no way, no how could he know about Jamie, right? Then again, his family has a cottage here, so maybe . . .

"You look beautiful," Trevor says and bends to give me a kiss. I turn my head so it lands on my cheek. I have no idea why this guy thinks he has the right to kiss me on the mouth. I've been on like two dates with him and certainly have no plans to go on any more, despite what my father wants.

"The new deck looks great, Kylee." He turns to me. "Who did you say you hired to do it?"

"I didn't," I say, and as my stomach twists, I glance at the clock. I need to text Jamie, let him know my father is in town. I reach for my phone, and my father places his hand over mine.

"Who did you hire?" he asks, his voice harder, his cold blue eyes locked on mine.

I shrug. "A local company. Blue Bay Construction. No one you would know."

My father's gaze lifts, and his eyes go dark as he exchanges a look with Trevor, a silent discussion that tells me there is more going on here. Unease trickles through my veins, and my thoughts go back to all the times I felt I was being watched . . . stalked. I have the sudden suspicion that my father had everything to do with it. Something foreboding creeps down my spine, and a hot ball of fury burns in my stomach.

"How long are you staying?" I ask my father, working to stay calm. A model of restraint, like my father would expect.

"Not long, I suspect." As I work to interpret that, he rubs his stomach. "What do you say we head out for a bite to eat? Go somewhere we can talk, get caught up."

"I can cook," I say, feeling a little unsteady on my feet. What's really going on here?

"No, I don't want to put you through the trouble," my father says, his voice hard, firm. "Besides, Trevor here is meeting his brothers at the local pub, Winchesters." He gives me a wink. "I'm sure you'll want to get to know his family. Someday they'll be your family."

Seriously!

Did he seriously just say that? Anger erupts inside me, and I'm about to protest when my dad's phone rings. He pulls it from his pocket and steps outside, leaving me alone with

Trevor, who looks different outside the office. Today's he's dressed in khaki shorts and a polo, and something niggles in the back of my mind. But it's too far out of reach for me to grasp it.

"I like what you've done with the place," Trevor says, glancing around. "Your new deck looks great."

"Thanks," I mumble and grab my purse. Since I know my father is not going to give in and let me out of dinner, the sooner I get it over with the better. I rush outside, and Trevor follows.

"I'll meet you there," I say and jump into my own car. I shoot a text off to Jamie so he doesn't just walk into my cottage and crawl into bed with me after he finishes at the tattoo shop, like he normally does.

I take off, and Dad follows along in his rental. We both park and when we enter the pub, I see three guys seated around the table and assume they're Trevor's brothers. Trevor puts his arm around my back to lead me to the table, and I try to shrug him off, but he's not deterred. He pulls a chair out for me and all eyes turn my way when I sit.

"Kylee, I'd like you to meet my brothers, Simon, Paxton, and Noah. Noah and Paxton are former SEALs, they're now working for your father."

"Oh," I say. "Really?"

"That's right," my dad says. "They've been doing some surveillance and investigative work."

My stomach recoils. Had one of these men been watching me?

"Simon is a lawyer," Trevor says. "And we're trying to lure him to your father's firm."

Simon flashes his teeth at me and I plaster on a smile and work to exchange pleasantries with these men. I take them in and rack my brain, trying to figure out why Noah looks so familiar. But my thoughts are a chaotic mess, flustered to find my intrusive father at my door and the man he's determined to marry me off to.

Over my dead body!

My father gestures to Stacy, and when the door bangs open behind me, all heads turn toward the sunlight filtering in. I suck in a breath when Jamie walks in with Tyler, Sean, and Ryan. He goes instantly still when he sees me at a table with my dad, Trevor, and his brothers. His knuckles fist, turn white, and his murderous eyes lock on mine. His nostrils flare and I can feel the anger rising up inside him. What the hell? I sent him a text letting him know I was having dinner with Dad and a colleague. Why does he look like he's about to kill someone? Did he not get my message? Does he think I have something going on with one of these guys?

A seed of hope blooms inside me at my last thought. If that's the case and he's jealous, that means he does care about me, and there is more going on between us than just sex. I smile at him, but his eyes go ocean cold and freeze the blood in my veins.

Jamie steps forward, like an indomitable force about to storm the castle. Threatening. Lethal. A total warrior. His three brothers, all enraged, keep tight on his heels as he inches forward, and I straighten in my chair, the hairs on the back of my neck standing on edge.

"Jamie," Trevor's brother Noah says and finishes the beer in his glass. It hits the table with a bang so loud, I nearly jump from my chair.

"Noah," Jamie responds through clenched teeth as the muscles in his jaw tick.

What the hell is going on? How do these guys know each other? Then again, Trevor and his family have summered here since they were kids—which is how Dad found out about the place—so I guess they must have known each other from their childhood.

"I see you finally found your way back to Blue Bay," Noah says. "Maybe you should have stayed in New Orleans." He grins and cracks his knuckles. "Safer for you there, don't you think?"

Jamie scoffs. "Why were you in my brother's house?" he asks.

Noah shrugs. "Who says I was?"

Sleek and solid, hard as steel, Jamie hovers, his fists clenching and unclenching. "What were you doing? Trying to dig up dirt? Get one of us thrown in jail?"

My mind is spinning, racing out of control as I work to sort through what is happening.

"Something like that."

"Find anything?" he asks, his voice lower, anger emanating from his every pore. "Or you just going to make shit up again?"

Noah slides a cool look my way, then turns back to Jamie. "You've been sleeping with my brother's *fiancé,* and that's a fact, pal."

So someone had been following me . . . and Jamie.

I gasp at that, and my father goes stiff beside me. I shoot him a glance and he's glaring at me, his eyes like granite, warning me to stay silent. But I've been silent enough. He had no right to put one of his men on me, follow me around, and watch my every move.

"Dad," I begin, but shut my mouth when Jamie speaks.

"I'm not your fucking pal. You call me that again, and it will be the last time," he says. He sucks in a sharp breath, his murderous eyes shooting daggers as they turn to me. "Fiancé? What is he talking about, Kylee?" he asks, his tone hard, bitter, rough-edged with something dangerous lurking just below the surface.

"Kylee is marrying my brother, douchebag," Noah says.

"Do you need me to use smaller words and shorter sentences for you to understand?"

Jamie takes a step toward Noah, and Noah jumps to his feet. Beck, the owner of the pub, and a good friend of the Owens boys, comes from his office in the back. He has only one rule in his place: No fighting.

"Outside," Jamie growls, and the sound reverberates through me. Is this really happening? Jamie is going to fight Trevor's brother in the parking lot?

I stand and make a move to go to Jamie, but my father grabs my wrist and stops me. I fall back into my chair, my heart thundering in my ears as the world as I know it comes at me a million miles an hour.

"I'm not interested in fighting you again, Jamie. Besides, do you really want another beating?"

Jamie's boots scrape as he steps closer and stands nose to nose with Noah, fearless. "Let's just make it a fair fight this time."

"Maybe another time."

Jamie jerks his thumb over his shoulder. "What, when my brothers aren't here?"

"Look, I'm just here to make sure you stay away from my brother's girl."

Jamie glances at me, searing possession in his gaze. "She's not his girl. You're fucking lying," Jamie counters, and I try to speak, but my father puts his hand on my arm and squeezes to stop me. My gaze shoots to his, then goes back to eyes the color of stirred-up sea during a raging summer storm.

"She never mentioned Trevor?" Paxton pipes in.

"No, she didn't, and you're all full of shit."

"If you don't believe me, ask her," Paxton says.

Jamie angles his head, and when his gaze lands on mine and I see the hurt, my heart misses a beat. I need to fix this and I need to do it now. No way can I let him think I'd been lying to him all this time, or that I betrayed his trust and what I *know* was growing between us.

"Jamie, it's not what you think," I manage to get out until my father squeezes my arm harder. "Oww," I say.

Jamie glares at my dad. "Let her go."

My father grins, unafraid. But dammit, he should be afraid. He should be very afraid of Jamie Owens and the army at his back.

"What, did you really think she loved you or something?" Simon says, as he twists his ring. I look down and nearly fall from my chair when I see the eagle etched into the gold. My gaze shoots to the scar on Jamie's chin. "Come on, Jamie. She was slumming, having a little fun before she went back to Atlanta to work for her daddy and marry my brother. Surely you knew that."

I shake my head. "Jamie . . ."

"Why all the trips to Hope Falls?" he asks, and in that instant, the clues register, and I realize why Noah is so familiar. He's the guy I saw in Hope Falls when I was with Summer, the guy she called Jackinoff. Understanding hits. The Jackson brothers are the Jackinoffs, and there is something very personal going on between these two families.

"Let me explain," I say quickly.

"One question. Is Trevor the guy you've been texting?"

My head is spinning so fast it's hard to keep a straight thought. "I . . . yes . . . but he's not . . . let me explain—"

"No, let me explain, Kylee," Trevor begins. "This is the man who raped our sister years ago." Trevor turns to my Dad. "Sorry, Jack, when I suggested this place for Kylee, I never thought this rapist asshole would be back causing trouble."

The bottom falls out of my world and I spin so fast, the room blurs before me. Jamie is glaring at me, his eyes dark, dangerous, deadly, and I shrink into myself, never having seen this side of him before. "Oh, my God, Jamie, is that true?"

Jamie dips his head, his pupils so dilated all I can see is black. He looks at me long and hard, then shakes his head. "What does the girl think?"

Before I can tell him what the *girl* thinks—what I, Kylee Jensen think—he turns around, offering me his back. But before he walks out the door, his brothers at his side, he says, "Goodbye, Kylee." And just like that, he saunters out the door, taking my shattered heart with him as he dismisses me from his life.

I'm about to stand, go after him, get to the bottom of matters, but the Jackson brothers and my father suddenly surround me. They're guiding me to the door, to my car.

"I need to talk to Jamie."

"He's no good, Kylee," my father says as he urges me inside my Lexus. "I want you to go back to the cottage and pack up. It's time to go home."

But I am home.

Numb all over, I slide into my car and catch the glint in Simon's eye as he twists his ring. My stomach turns, and bile punches into my throat. I want to run after Jamie. I need to talk to him.

Jamie raped their sister?

The Jamie I know is kind, gentle, so sweet and caring. Something is off here. I feel it in my bones. I'm about to jump from my vehicle when my father slams my door shut and I catch the look in Simon's eyes, warning me there will be trouble if I do. I grip the steering wheel and stare straight ahead, catch the tail end of Jamie's bike as he exits the parking lot, leaving me, and what was between us behind. I have no idea what to believe anymore, but I do know that if I don't do as my father says, it could put Jamie at risk.

16

JAMIE

It's been two long weeks since Kylee packed her bags and headed back to Atlanta with her father and her fiancé. Was she really having an affair with me while planning to marry one of the douchebag Jackinoff assholes? Fuck, could my life be any more of a mess?

Running on empty, completely lost without her, I sit on my bike outside Gram's house, no desire to go to work today. With the deep pain of loss leaving me drained, all I want to do is drink myself to sleep and curl up on my own fucking misery. Gram comes from the front door, a load of containers in her hands. Last night's leftovers. She slides them into the back of the truck and heads inside to get the rest. I throw my leg over the bike and take the stairs two at a time to help her. She's a bit breathless when she comes back out, meeting me on the porch, and I look her over.

"Are you okay, Gram?"

"The heat is getting to me," she says.

Worry gnaws at me. She hasn't quite been herself since Kylee left and I've been doing nothing but basking in my own shithole misery when I should have been paying closer attention to her health. "Why don't I drive you to Hope Falls and help out?"

Gram touches my cheek. "Such a sweet boy."

I swallow at the gesture, my mind once again returning to Kylee and the endearments she used with me. I still can't fucking believe she thought I could rape someone. That she actually fucking asked me if it was true. After everything we've done, the intimacies we shared, when it came right down to it, she didn't believe me, or believe in me.

She believed in you enough to help with the tattoo shop.

What the fuck ever.

When it came to the important things, like thinking I was a rapist, she questioned me, and that spoke volumes. I should have kept my fucking dick in my pants. Haven't I learned that rich pampered girls only like to play games with boys from the wrong side of the tracks? We're not the kind of guys they bring home to Daddy, and I was a stupid asshole for thinking we had something of value, something that went beyond the bedroom. I hadn't seen much of Kylee before she upped and left, I'd been too busy tearing down a wall at the tattoo shop and adding an extension, using money I didn't have. Now it was all for nothing.

I feel like total shit, and the truth is, two months ago, I might have said I didn't care what anyone thought of me, but that was bullshit. I cared what Kylee thought, and I thought she believed in me. When will I ever fucking learn where rich pampered girls are concerned?

Yeah, I've been down this road, but this time it hurt more, because back when I was a kid it wasn't real love. No, what I had with Kylee was deep, meaningful, something that *forevers* are built on. A dark sound catches in my throat. Yeah, well, let me rephrase . . . what I *thought* I had with Kylee was deep, meaningful, something *forevers* are built on—or not.

What a stupid son of a bitch.

Who now sports a broken fucking heart.

Fuck me.

I finish carrying the containers to the truck and help Gram into the passenger seat. Her face is flushed and anger morphs to worry. "You sure you're okay?"

She waves me away. "I will be," she says. "When it all works out."

Even though I have no idea what she means by that, I drive to Hope Falls. I park outside the shelter and help her bring the containers inside. The second we enter, my heart falls into my stomach, my breath leaving my lungs in a loud whoosh.

No. Fucking. Way.

Gram is watching me, studying me closely, and I shake my head, incredulous

"I'm the one who should be asking if you're okay," she says. "You look like you've seen a ghost."

"I . . ." When I take in all the women and kids and see most of them are dressed in Kylee's designer clothes, I stumble a bit. Gram reaches for me, but I sag against the wall and bend forward. With my hands braced on my knees I take deep gulping breaths and try to wrap my brain around this unexpected turn of events.

This . . . this is what she was doing in Hope Falls? Secretly outfitting the needy with clothes and telling no one about it. Here I thought she was meeting Trevor—I basically accused her of that—keeping her fiancé a secret from me when she was helping others.

I am such an asshole for questioning her. I briefly pinch my eyes shut, barely able to hold on to the control fighting against the pain inside me. How could I have done that to her?

"What have I done?" I say to myself.

"It's not what you've done, it's what you're going to do next," Gram says. "If you love her, you'll fight for her."

Fight for her? I want to fight for her. Fuck, I want to fight for the love burning so deep inside of me I fear it's going to consume me whole. But how can I? "Gram, she thought I raped her fiancé's sister."

"Fiancé?"

"Yeah, she's engaged to Trevor Jackson." I shake my head, gut-wrenching anger tearing me up inside. "I know she did a good thing here, but the bottom line is she's no different from any other rich, pampered girl. I never should have let myself believe she was."

"You didn't, Jamie. You didn't let yourself believe it. Not once."

"What are you talking about?"

Gram puts her hand on my face. "Sweet boy, if you thought she was different, you wouldn't have been trying to hide your relationship and wouldn't have kept secrets from her. You did it because you were hurt deeply and weren't about to risk your heart by putting it on the line again. Deep down, you expected the worst from her, because of who she is and where she comes from. You set yourself up for failure, Jamie."

I tense and a shiver rakes up my back at her blunt words. I struggle to find a flaw in her reasoning. "She's engaged, Gram."

Green eyes narrow, "Are you sure about that?"

A numbing sensation settles deep into my bones. "That's what all the guys said."

"They also said you raped their sister, and you didn't. Did Kylee come out and tell you she was engaged?"

The knot in my throat thickens. "No, but she jumped all over me."

"Did you defend yourself?"

I scoff. "I didn't bother."

"Why not?"

Anxiety prickles across my skin as old insecurities and fears rush to the surface. "Because I—"

Motherfucker.

Bile punches into my throat. Gram is right. I set myself up for disaster. I never bothered explaining because deep inside I believed she'd never see me as good enough, rich enough, or anything other than a criminal. I never gave sweet Kylee the benefit of the doubt. Good thing I'm not the lawyer in our relationship.

Relationship.

Yeah, I fucking want a relationship with Kylee. I'm miserable without her. But what can I do? I ruined everything when I turned my back on her and let her walk out of Blue Bay. Dumbass motherfucker that I am.

The room grows so quiet you could hear a pin drop, then Gram breaks the silence by asking, "Are you really going to lose the best thing that's ever happened to you because of past mistakes?" I run my hand through my hair, and Gram continues. "You're going to have to open up to her, Jamie. Fully. Lay your heart out for her, and trust in her enough to believe she's not going to shatter it."

My mind races, sorting through the facts. Is she engaged or not? Did she believe in me or not? What's real? What isn't?

As I consider that, my galloping heart settles inside my overly tight chest, because deep inside it, I know the real truth—and because of that, I need my cousin Ryan.

17

KYLEE

I miss Jamie.

I miss him with all my heart, and there isn't a damn thing I can do about it. He walked out of my life and didn't so much as give me one last glance goodbye. As I think about things now, I'm not even sure I could have made things right if I'd gone after him.

I sit at my office desk in Atlanta and look out my rain-streaked window, as tears and grief threaten to consume me. I hate it here. I hate everything about this building, my work, my colleagues—especially Trevor and his brothers. I miss Blue Bay—a place I truly felt I belonged.

Home.

I close my eyes to pinch off tears. Did Jamie really think I was the kind of woman who'd sleep with him if I were engaged to another man? I guess I should have told him about Trevor. Then again, there were things he should have told me too.

Do I really think he's the kind of man who'd rape a woman? We both had secrets, and in the heat of the moment, I asked if it was true, but it was a knee-jerk reaction. So much was going on and I was frightened as the men faced off against each other, frightened to realize it was Trevor and his brothers who beat Jamie and left him deeply scarred, inside and out.

Jamie is a good man, the bravest man I know, and I hurt him so deeply by questioning him, not believing in him—the only thing he ever wanted from those who loved him. I bite back a gut-wrenching sob. After everything he'd been through, he showed me a kindness and gentleness that gave me such respect for him. The need I feel for him curls through my bloodstream. A noise sounds at my door and I glance up to see Trevor. Weary, I quickly swipe away the tears and straighten in my seat.

"How's your day going?" he asks.

"Good," I say and grab a file, any file from my desk, even though I haven't been able to concentrate on anything since I came to work early. I didn't have to officially start for a couple more weeks, but all I was doing at home was moping around in misery.

"Want to grab lunch?" he asks.

"No, I have plans," I say, lying. Why is this man still pursuing me after finding out I was sleeping with his number-one enemy? That thought gives me pause. What's in it for him?

"Can you break them?" he asks and comes farther into my office. He straightens his tie, and I get a whiff of his expensive cologne as he moves closer.

"No," I say.

"Kylee. Look at me." His voice is firm, a little demanding, and it totally reminds me of my father.

I lift my head, chills moving along my spine. "What?"

"Why are you making this so hard?" he asks, changing tactics by softening his tone. Does he really think that's going to work with me?

"Making what hard, Trevor?" Needing to occupy my hands before I get up and choke him, I grab a pen and tap it on my desk.

He waves his hand back and forth between the two of us. "This. Us. Don't you realize we'd be a power couple around here? We'd move up the ladder together." He shakes his head. "Together . . . we could do so many things . . . even make partnership."

"So that's what this is about, then, a promotion for you?"

"That's how life works, Kylee."

I think about Jamie. That's not how things work in his life. He was true, honest, not a manipulative bone in his body. He didn't sleep with me for any other reason than he wanted to—he wanted me. A little thrill goes through me, but then sadness moves in when I realize I'll never see him again.

"Why do you love law?" I ask, and push back in my seat.

His look is confused at first, then he says, "The power, the money, prestige. I'm sure your reasons are the same."

Where was the passion? The love of helping others?

"Then you'd be wrong."

"Come on, Kylee. Don't tell me you're still hung up on that rapist asshole."

My spine stiffens, anger boiling my blood. "He didn't rape your sister," I say through gritted teeth.

"And you know that how?" He walks up to my desk, puts his palms on it, and leans forward.

"I just do."

"I know what the records say, that my sister lied, but that's bullshit."

I take a moment to mull that over. "I didn't read the records. I didn't need to." I touch my heart. "I know it in here."

"Well, he left you, remember? It's over, and now it's time to think about me and you." He taps his head. "You need to be smart about your future. That guy can't offer you the things I can."

Before I even realize what he's doing, he comes around to the side of the desk and goes down on one knee. He reaches into his jacket and produces a velvet box.

I jump to my feet and my chair hits the wall behind me. I stand there, completely shocked, the room closing in on me. I gulp down a mouthful of air, unable to believe he's proposing.

"Marry me, Kylee. We'll make a great team."

A great team? Another wave of anger takes hold. Marriage isn't just about making a great team. While teamwork is important, marriage is about love, respect, truth, taking pleasure in the person's successes, being there in the good times and bad, and helping that other person be the best they can be. They way Jamie supported my dream of being a designer and helped me be the best person I could be. Honest to God, the man messed with my life so thoroughly, how could I have thought for one second that I could go back to this? How could I let a man like that walk out of my life without a fight?

My gaze lifts when I see movement in my doorway, and I take in my father as well as Trevor's brothers. My father has a huge smile of his face.

"Of course she says yes," he bursts out, his eyes narrowing in on me, as if he's daring me to say no. As I look at him, my heart races. I think about Jamie and his bravery, the way his father was always there for him and supported his passions by getting a tattoo. In that moment, I do what Trevor says and use my brains to think things over, figure out what's important and what isn't. I think about how hard I worked for my law degree, the years I've invested to make my own father happy, the lengths I'd go to be his obedient daughter, just for an ounce of his love, respect . . . and time. As I consider all that, a plan forms, takes shape, and I feel a new measure of calm.

"Answer him," my father says.

I inhale a shaky breath and release it slowly as I warm to the idea bouncing around inside my brain. "I will," I say and look at the man on his knees before me.

18

JAMIE

I drop the roller brush after putting the last touches on the expansion and shrug out of my coveralls. I crack a window to let a breeze in and stand back to look at my handiwork, pleased with the way the room turned out. My mind goes to Kylee, and my pulse beats double-time. I run my hand over my chest, pausing near my heart—where Kylee will forever exist.

Now that the room is finished, I have one thing left to do, and nothing or no one is going to stop me or stand in my way. The bell over my door rings and I turn, about to let whoever just came in know that we're not open. But when I see Kylee standing there, an uneasy look on her face, my heart jumps into my throat and the room spins before my eyes.

"Kylee . . ." I manage to get past the peach-size lump as my heart thunders in my ears, hardly able to believe she's here. I pray to fucking God I'm not hallucinating. "What . . . are you doing here?"

Casually, and with a little sway to her hips, she walks into the shop and runs her hands over my things. She's working hard to appear brave and calm, but I know her well enough to know she's as shaken up as I am.

Is she really here?

"I was thinking," she says and climbs into my tattoo chair. "That you should ink me."

I soak in her words, see need flashing in her eyes, and try to wrap my brain around the fact that the girl I'm in love with is back in Blue Bay. Sitting in my chair, nonetheless.

"You really want ink?" I ask, my stomach coiled so tight, I feel sick. Is she here for sex, or more?

My thoughts fall off when she widens her legs. "Right here. Our little secret."

"I hate secrets," I say, my heart sinking into my stomach.

"Me too." Sadness moves over her face, and beneath the act I see the sweet, vulnerable girl I fell in love with. She frowns. "They can lead to all kinds of problems."

I step up to her, needing to know where this is going, what she wants from me. If she doesn't want what I want, what the fuck will I do? How will I go on?

"What are you thinking?" I ask and touch her thigh. A hot flush crawls up her neck and she practically vibrates beneath me.

"This guy once told me he'd like to give me the Viking symbol."

My heart tightens with the love I feel for her. I draw a slow steady breath to collect myself. "Is that what you really want?"

"I trust that guy. If he thinks I should have a Viking symbol, then I should have a Viking symbol."

I narrow my eyes and let my gaze race over her pretty face. She doesn't look like she slept any more than I did these last few weeks. I touch her cheek and she leans into my hand.

"You remember what it means?" I ask quietly, hoping like

hell she does, and that what she's really trying to tell me is she's ready to create her own life and a future with me.

She puts her hand over mine, a small sound of contentment catching in her throat. "Yes."

"Ink is permanent," I say, inching closer.

"I know," she whispers, her warm breath falling over my face.

"So if I put the symbol here," I begin, and run my fingers over her thighs, "does it mean you're interested in creating your own reality?"

"Yes," she says, and my heart beats so hard, I'm sure it's going to break a rib. Hope moves through me, and in this instance, I know if I want a future with her, I need to lay my heart on the line. Am I ready for that? Hell yeah, I am. This is sweet Kylee Jensen, and I wouldn't trust my heart in anyone's hands but hers.

"Kylee," I begin. "I never raped—"

She puts her finger to my lips to hush me. "I know."

I frown as old painful memories bombard me. But that's what they are now. Memories. It's time to live in the present and not let the past define my actions. "I take it you looked up the court case."

"No. I didn't need to." The lump in my throat doubles in size.

"Really?" I choke out. She didn't need to read the case to believe in me?

"I believe you, Jamie. I believe in you."

"You didn't at first."

It was a knee jerk reaction. Everything was coming at me fast and my rational brain went right to the facts: you did something wrong, which is why the guys beat you up. But it didn't feel right in my gut, even as I asked the question."

"They beat me up because they thought I raped their sister. There isn't one of my brothers who wouldn't do the same, but they all jumped me when I was alone. None of us would have done that."

"I'm so sorry they did that to you." She touches my hair pushes it from my face. "For the record, I was never engag—"

This time I put my finger to her lips. "I know. The truth is, I was hurt in the past, deeply. I was accused of a crime I didn't commit by a rich, pampered girl who was bored and looking for fun. I put you in that category, didn't expect you to be any different. But you proved to be so different, and I totally fell in love with you."

"You . . . you love me?" she says, and sniffs.

I shake my head. "Of course I love you."

She looks down for a second, a moment of silence, then says, "I'm not here to tell you all the things I love about you, Jamie."

I freeze, the blood in my veins turning to ice. I glance over her face as I inch back. My stomach turns, worry gnawing at me. "What do you mean?" Oh, fuck, does she not want to try to make this work between us? I can't let that happen. I have to find a way to convince her we're meant to be together. Walking away from her was the stupidest thing I've ever done, and I refuse to lose her again. She's mine. She was mine from the second I looked at her lounging in her bikini. Yeah, she was trouble in a bikini, all right—my trouble —and I plan to fight for her.

"Jamie," she begins. "I'm here to tell you all the things I don't love about you," she whispers.

Fear flashes through me, and I let loose a long, slow breath to prepare myself for what she's about to say to me. I move back on shaky legs, but she captures my hand and pulls me back beside her.

"I don't love you because you're the bravest, kindest guy I know." I swallow, and when understanding dawns, I slide my hand around her neck, the happiest fucking man alive. "I don't love you because you're talented, passionate, and really and truly care about other people." She gives me a small smile and my insides soar. "I don't love you because you overstepped boundaries and went to Indigo Blue Boutique. I don't love you because you put me first, care about me, support my true passion in life."

"Kylee," I whisper my heart overflowing with all the love I feel for her.

She presses a soft kiss onto my mouth. "I love you because this summer you became my best friend, and you make me brave."

"I love you, Kylee," I say and nearly sob with the happiness bubbling up inside me. "I don't ever want to lose you again." I pull her into my arms, and hug her until she's gasping for breath. "I was so stupid to walk away, but I swear to you, I won't let anything ever come between us again."

"Trevor asked me to marry him."

Ice goes through my veins, never wanting to hear that man's name on her lips again. I inch back to see her face. When our eyes connect and I see the grief, I stiffen. "And?"

"My father said yes for me."

I grab a fistful of hair and tug. My pulse stutters. If we love each other, how the fuck could this be happening? "Jesus Christ."

"After my father answered for me, he demanded I answer Trevor too, and I told him, I will."

The room spins around me and I grip the side of my tattoo chair to hang on. "You will? As in you will marry him?"

"No, as in I will answer him. And the answer was no, of course."

I exhale a sharp breath. "Fuck, you scared me for a second there."

Her gaze races over mine, and while I see love in her eyes,

I also see fear and worry. "I left my job, and my father has practically disowned me."

"He'll come around, Kylee. When he sees you truly happy that you are making your own clothes, he'll come around."

"Maybe," she says. "I'm so sorry for what the Jackson brothers did to you. If they ever come after you because of me—"

"Let them. You're worth the fight."

"But Jamie—"

"Kylee, they jumped me. It wasn't a fair fight. I was a kid and still managed to break a few of their bones. They come at me again, they'll have me and my army of brothers and cousins to deal with."

She nods and I take her hand and lift her from the chair. I walk her into the room I just finished painting. "This is where we go."

She looks around the new add-on. "What is this?"

"This is why I was barely around last month. I was adding an extension, for you."

"For me?"

"Yeah, I want you to open your own boutique right here, attached to the tattoo shop. That way we can be together." I wink and add, "I'd even let you hum."

She grins but then she shakes her head. "Jamie, I can't believe you did this."

"I'd do anything for you."

Her eyes are wide as she takes it all in. "I'm going to need help."

"I'll help you."

She puts her hand on my chest and I close mine over it. "You'll be busy doing your own work. I was thinking I'd like to hire a friend."

"Oh, who?"

"Miranda. I know her from . . ."

". . . the shelter," I say.

Her eyes go wide. "You know her?"

"She wears your clothes well." There is real warmth in her eyes when she realizes I know all about her trips to Hope Falls. "I want permanent," I say.

"I thought ink was the only permanent thing in your life," she teases.

I take my shirt off and when her gaze goes to my heart, and the word Kylee written over it—compliments of Ryan— she covers her mouth with her hand. "I was coming for you, Kylee. I was just getting everything ready before I went to Atlanta to convince you we belong together."

I wrap my arms around her and pull her tight. Tears are streaming down her face and I kiss them away. "I was thinking, we could hang a sign and call the place Body Art, because you know, you put clothes on the body and I put tattoos on it, and they're both art."

The happiness in her eyes makes me feel more alive than I have ever felt before. "Or we could just call it Jamie and Kylee's Place."

"Better yet, how about Owens and Owens?"

Her eyes go big and she squeals. "Jamie . . ."

"Marry me, Kylee. Make me the happiest man in the world."

"On one condition," she says, her voice teasing.

I angle my head, take in her mischievous grin. "You have a condition?"

She turns from me, gives a little shake to her backside and says, "You said you wanted to take me everywhere, and that hasn't happened yet."

"Jesus fuck," I say.

She grins at me over her shoulder. "Exactly."

I scoop her up. "Not here. Let's take you home, and I'll give you anything and everything you want."

Home.

My God, I'm really going to make a home with Kylee Jensen. I am the luckiest fucking man alive.

"Oh, and I also want a dog or two, and at least five kids or more. We can't stop until we get Gram her girl. And we'll need to expand the cottage to make room for everyone, and—"

I laugh. "You can have all those things, but for now, can we just start with me putting my cock inside you?"

"Whatever you say, sweet boy."

"Sweet boy? Haven't we been over that?"

She blinks, feigning innocence. "I don't remember."

"Maybe the girl needs a reminder of just how not sweet I am," I say, slipping into our game, not because I want to keep an emotional distance. I don't. But just because this fantasy has become a reality, it doesn't mean the good girl doesn't want to be a little bad.

She smiles at me. "I believe the girl does."

Thank You!

Thank you so much for reading, **Leveled**, book a in my Blue Bay Crew Series. I hope you loved this story as much as I loved writing it. Be sure to keep reading for an excerpt of **Single Dad Next Door.**

Interested in leaving a review? Please do! Reviews help readers connect with books that work for them. I appreciate all reviews, whether positive or negative.

Happy Reading,

Cathryn

SINGLE DAD NEXT DOOR

Rachel

When my bedroom door flies open and crashes hard against the paint-chipped wall, I groan. "Go away," I say, my voice muffled by my pillow. Not that my roommates will listen, even if they can hear me. Heck, I could scream at the top of my lungs and it wouldn't faze them, much less send them running back to their rooms —not when the view outside my window is that *hot*.

Seriously though, sharing a house with four college freshmen is not my idea of a good time, not when I'm a senior and working my ass off to get into law school. But when I left NYU two months before the start of my fourth year and transferred to Penn State at the last minute, this place was all I could find—and afford. Ultimately, Penn State is where I want to do my law degree after undergrad. I just ended up here sooner, rather than later.

Someone tugs at my pillow and I open one eye to see Becca hovering over me. "Come on, Rach, he just took his shirt off," she says. "You're going to want to see this."

Why oh why did my room have to come with the best view of the hot neighbor's driveway?

"Thank God for this heat wave." Sylvie, roommate number two, fans her face with her hand.

I groan and curl up into the fetal position. I just want one more minute in bed without every member of the house in my room. "I. Don't. Care." Well, that might be a lie. I like looking at the eye candy next door as well as they do, but after putting in a late night at Pizza Villa—I seriously have to find a new job—I need all the sleep I can get before class.

"Jesus, would you look at him," Becca says, her voice a breathy whisper as she peers out the window. "Talk about slurpalicious. I could seriously lick that from head to toe, and back up again."

"Leave," I say on a yawn.

Ignoring me, Sylvie squeals. "He's going back into his garage. Damned if he doesn't look as good going as he does coming."

"But I'd rather see him...*coming*," Becca says, and they start giggling.

"Seriously. Are you both twelve?"

"Shh, he's back," Becca says and swats her hand at me, like I'm an annoying fly that needs to be shooed away.

I shift on my bed, not to get a better look outside my window. No, moving has absolutely nothing at all to do with the shirtless mechanic turning my roommates into dim-witted moths. The *only* reason I'm getting up is to herd these girls from my room, and if I happen to get a glimpse of the hot, tattooed, badass daddy next door, well...then so be it.

I rub the blur from my eyes and toss my pillow at them. "Get away from my window, before he thinks it's me." They don't need to know that the hottie's bedroom window is also across from mine, and that late one night, he caught me staring into his room as he walked around in nothing but boxer shorts. Heck, if they knew that, they'd camp out for the rest of the school year, and that was so not happening.

"Ohmigod!" Sylvie leaps back. "I think he just saw me." She puts her hand over her mouth and starts to giggle. Footsteps pound down the hall, announcing the arrival of my other two roommates. I shake my head as they come bursting in.

Kill. Me. Now.

"Is he out there?" Val asks, her big blue eyes wide and hopeful.

"Yeah, but he saw me looking," Sylvie says. Despite that, she edges back around to sneak another look. Megan hurries across the room, and goes up on her toes to peer over Sylvie's shoulder, trying to catch a glimpse without getting caught.

"Do you really think he killed someone?" Megan asks.

"That's the rumor," Val protests, though her tone holds uncertain convictions.

"Then why isn't he in jail?"

"Maybe it was self-defense."

"He's such a badass."

"He's good with his little girl, though."

"Bad Boy Daddy, now that's hot."

"Do you think he'd spank me if I was bad?"

Unable to put up with their incessant chatter and giggles any longer, I point my finger toward the door. "Out. Now."

A chorus of grumbles ensues as they all sullenly walk to my door. Christ, I'm getting that lock fixed, even if I have to eat ramen noodles for the next month.

"God, you're such a grouch in the morning." Becca shoots me a wounded look over her shoulder.

"Doesn't even have to be the morning," Val adds with a hair toss.

"You need to get your nose out of a book once in a while," Megan says.

"What she needs is to get laid," Sylvie informs them all, but her solution to pretty much everything is sex. Problem is, this time Megan is nodding her head in sad agreement as she follows Sylvie out the door.

"I can hear you," I shout after them. I shake my head and my mussed hair falls over my shoulders. "I'm still right here." As I stand there, dressed only in my tank top and underwear, a warm breeze blows in and slides over my skin, a late reminder that I'd opened my window last night before crawling into bed exhausted. Great. Not only could the hot guy working on his car see my roommates drooling over him, he could *hear* them as well. *And* they just announced that I needed to get laid. How freaking mortifying. I stomp across the room and yell down the hall, "And don't bother to close my door on your way out." As usual my sarcasm is ignored.

I give the door a good slam, which helps improve my mood a little. With a deep breath, I turn around, not to see my hot neighbor, but to close my window. No way do I want him hearing anything else that goes on inside this place, or get the wrong idea that I might want him. I don't. Not in a million years.

I'm completely off guys, trying to keep a low profile. After my ex-boyfriend turned violent and abusive, threatening to kill me if I went to the police, I snuck away under the cover of darkness and put several states between us. He was big and hard like my neighbor, his muscles born from rough carpentry work. Last year, when he came to do repairs on the house I was sharing with friends, I was flattered that I was the object of his attention. At first he was doting and attentive, but as time went by, he became possessive and controlling. I came to find out later, he'd had other charges against him from numerous other women.

Jesus, why am I such a bad judge of character when it comes to men. Oh, probably because my only role model had been a mean-assed, alcoholic father who drove my beautiful, caring mom to an early grave and me out of the house the second I turned eighteen.

If I try hard enough I can still smell the cheap perfume on his shirt when he stumbled in after a weekend-long drinking binge. God, how I hated those women he slept around with almost as much as I hated my Dad. Mom used to try to protect me from his disgusting behavior, but what hurt the most was how he dragged Mom down, aging her pretty face far too early.

My heart squeezes as I think about her. She was a good woman, but was too afraid to leave. Running is hard. I get that now. Not that she really had anywhere to run. Our only other relative was my father's mother. She's still alive, living in upstate Pennsylvania where my Dad was born. While she liked me well enough, when it came to Mom and Dad, she always took Dad's side. That's how it is with parents, I guess.

I lift my arms, place my hands on the frame, and lean in to give it a tug when the hottie slowly lifts his head. Our eyes meet, hold a moment too long, and I suck in a quick breath as heat zings through me—and dammit, it's not the autumn sun that has warmth pooling between my legs.

OMFG.

With a wrench clasped tightly in his right hand he stares at me, like we're in a goddamn Mexican standoff. I swallow hard, and will myself to move, but can't seem to tear my gaze away. Ah, what was that I said about dim-witted moths?

Close the window, Rachel.

While my brain struggles to call the shots, my body has other ideas. Ideas that involve staying exactly where I am and ogling the hottest guy I'd ever seen. Blue eyes, square jaw, a body I could play Plinko on, and low riding, well-worn jeans that accentuate bulges in all the right places, and holy hell, the man has a lot of right places. Want prowls through me, hitting every erogenous spot along the way.

Just shut the window already.

He shifts his stance and taps the wrench against his leg as he looks up at me. A small grin touches his mouth, and that's when I realize I'm half naked. *Please, ground, open up and swallow me.* After hearing the girls, he probably thinks I'm trying to lure him to my room, fix that dry spell I've been going through. I grip the window ledge tighter and slam it down, putting the brakes on my body's reaction, and shutting out six delicious feet of hard muscle and pure testosterone. This is so not what I need right now. Coffee. Yeah, that's what I need. Lots and lots of coffee.

I hurry to the kitchen and shove a pod into the Keurig. I pour milk into a cup and set it on the spill tray. As I wait for the coffee to percolate, I wander into the main level bathroom and glance in the mirror. I look at myself and try to imagine how I appeared through the blue-eyed mechanic's eyes. I see black smudges under tired eyes, boobs that only look big because I'm slender from work, school and lack of proper nutrition and rest. My hair is...wait... I grab a fistful of my curls and examine them closer. Oh, God, pizza sauce.

Could this day get any worse?

Christ, even if he did hear my roommates, I'm sure he'd never look twice at a girl like me—especially the way I look now. A guy like him probably goes out with women who are a little more put together, sexier. Although I have to say in the two months I've lived here, I've never seen a woman come or go from his place. Still, I'm certain a girl next door who always smells like marinara sauce and pepperoni isn't even on his radar.

Good, because I don't want to be.

The coffee machine beeps and I hurry back to the kitchen. I grab the mug to take a big sip. Heavenly. Desperate for a shower, to wash last night's work from my hair, I hurry back upstairs to my room, hot mug of coffee in hand. I check the time and grab my clothes. Giggles come from Sylvie's room across the hall as I dash into the bathroom. I turn the shower to cool, partly because it's just so hot in the house, and partly because I need to calm my overheated body down. I might be off men, especially big, scary ones like my neighbor, but my body and brain aren't working in sync this morning. Clearly my libido didn't get the memo when I left New York.

I stay under the needle-like spray longer than normal, needing an extra minute to clear my head. When the water turns cooler, I jump out, dry off, and pull on a pair of shorts and T-shirt. I towel dry my hair, then tie it back into a ponytail. I forgo makeup. Not only will it melt off my face, I'm not trying to impress anyone or draw any kind of attention to myself. Once done, I grab my purse, shove my textbooks into my backpack, and head for the front door, feeling a little more alive after the coffee.

The hot morning air hits like a slap in the face and I groan. It's October for God's sake. It's supposed to be time for pumpkin spiced lattes. This is more like beach weather. Mother nature needs to get her shit together. I glance at my watch, and judging by the time—thanks to an extra-long shower—I need to get my shit together, too. This morning I'll have to take my car to school, or risk being late for class. The walk to campus is long, around forty-five minutes, but I prefer it on days like today. I need to save my gas money for the colder winter months.

Since my driveway runs parallel to my neighbor's, I keep my head down, toss my backpack into the back seat and climb into the driver's side. Thank God the hottie is out of sight and I don't have to go through the embarrassment of facing him.

I roll my window down and shove the key into the ignition. I turn it, only for the engine to make some god-awful sound and stall out. My heart races quicker. Shit. Shit. Shit. Frustrated, I give the steering wheel a thump with my fist. This can't be happening. I need this car. Need to be able to depend on it if I have to run again. It might be an old junker, but it's all I have. I can't afford a new one. Heck, I'm on such a tight budget, I can't even afford to have this one fixed.

I take a deep breath, throw up a silent prayer, and twist the key again, only for it to cough and gasp, like it's dying a slow and painful death.

No. No. No

A tap comes on the roof, and I turn to see my hot—shirt-less—neighbor with his arms braced over the door of my car. He leans down, his beautiful face close to mine. "Need a hand?"

"I...uh...it's not working."

Jeez, way to state the obvious.

He grins, and when I see a cute dimple that contrasts sharply with his chiseled face, I nearly swallow my tongue.

"Yeah, I kind of got that, you know, being a mechanic and all." As he gives off a bad-boy vibe that messes with my common sense, he grabs a cloth from his back pocket, and wipes his hands before leaning into the car, his head practi-cally in my lap.

Holy fuck!

It takes everything, and I mean *everything*, in me not to grab the back of his head and shove it between my legs. My sex practically quivers at the visual. The girls were right. I do need to get laid. I bite the inside of my cheek to stifle the moan rising in my throat.

"What...what are you doing?" I finally manage to ask, and will myself not to writhe restlessly, and show him what a needy girl I really am.

He pulls the hood release, and the front end of my car jumps. His head lifts and once again his face is close to mine.

"Popping the hood." He angles his head, and his eyes narrow. "What did you think I was doing?"

Oh, I don't know. Maybe you were taking this opportunity to go down on me.

"Popping the hood," I say quickly, and try not to think of sex. Dirty sex. Take-me-up-against-the-wall kind of sex. Not that I know anything about that. Sadly.

His laugh is rough and deep as he walks around to the front of the car, and I unbuckle quickly. My legs wobble as I climb out of the driver's seat and follow him. He's grinning when I reach him.

"What?" I ask, my voice raspy.

He touches my cracked windshield washer cap, which I happened to repair all by myself. "Duct tape?" he asks, his voice amused.

"Tools of the trade, right," I say and try not to sound as breathless as I feel. A difficult task considering I'm standing next to a half-naked man that I want to run my hands all over. I mean I've seen shirtless guys before, but come on. This guy is like a freaking viking. He leans forward to fiddle with something, and the movement shows off impressive bicep muscles. I break a sweat as his closeness sends shudders of need between my thighs. Honest to God, the man is a work of art, and all I can think of is no-strings sex—something I've never done before. But that's crazy and reckless and so not me. Truthfully, if I knew what was good for me, I'd slam the hood shut and run in the opposite direction.

I'm about to do just that when he says, "Uh, huh."

"Is...is there something wrong?" Is that my voice? Christ, I sound like I'm whacked out on painkillers.

For God's sake, get it together, girl.

He rubs the scruff on his chin, and I step back, needing a measure of distance before I actually reach out and run my hands over all his hard grooves and deep valleys.

"Plenty," he says again and checks something else. I have no clue what he's doing. I only know that he looks as hot as hell doing it. As he leans over my car, my gaze slides to his ass, committing the way his pants cup his cheeks to memory. The guy could be in a jeans commercial, or better yet, a Calvin Klein underwear ad. I'm a girl, but advertising like that would have me one-clicking the buy button.

My heart hammers as he stands again. He turns toward me, but I'm far too slow to react. His eyes are piercing, almost a deeper shade of blue when my gaze jerks to his, and I can't tell whether he's thrilled or pissed to find me checking him out.

I step closer and look over the engine. "So, what is it?" I ask, disgusted with myself. I should not be fantasizing over this man.

He clears his throat. "I think the first thing we need to do is replace the spark plugs," he answers, his voice a little hoarse.

"Yeah, that's what I was thinking," I say, my head bobbing in agreement.

That grin is back when I look at him. "You know something about cars?"

I shrug. "Sure...and duck tape."

He laughs and says, "It's not..." he shakes his head. "Never mind. So, you agree then, that something's not firing right?"

Firing? Oh, things were firing all right, and lighting up my body like a goddamn Fourth of July celebration.

Damn him.

Damn Mother Nature.

Damn dim-witted moths.

Confessions of a Bad Boy Fighter

Confessions of a Bad Boy Gamer

Confessions of a Bad Boy Millionaire

Confessions of a Bad Boy Santa

Confessions of a Bad Boy CEO

Hands On

Hands On

Body Contact

Full Exposure

Dossier

Private Reserve

House Rules

Under Pressure

Big Catch

Brazilian Fantasy

Improper Proposal

Boys of Beachville

Good at Being Bad

Igniting the Bad Boy

Bad Girl Therapy

Stone Cliff Series:

Crashing Down

Wasted Summer

Love Lessons

Wrapped Up

Eternal Pleasure Series

Instinctive

Impulsive

Indulgent

Sun Stroked Series

Seaside Seduction

Deep Desire

Private Pleasure

Captured and Claimed Series:

Yours to Take

Yours to Teach

Yours to Keep

Firefighter Heat Series

Fever

Siren

Flash Fire

Playing For Keeps Series

Slow Ride

Wild Ride

Sweet Ride

Breaking the Rules:

Hold Me Down Hard

Pin Me Up Proper

Tie Me Down Tight

Stand Alone Title:

Hands on with the CEO

Torn Between Two Brothers

Holiday Spirit

Unleashed

Knocking on Demon's Door

Web of Desire

ABOUT CATHRYN

New York Times and *USA today* Bestselling author, Cathryn is a wife, mom, sister, daughter, and friend. She loves dogs, sunny weather, anything chocolate (she never says no to a brownie) pizza and red wine. She has two teenagers who keep her busy with their never ending activities, and a husband who is convinced he can turn her into a mixed martial arts fan. Cathryn can never find balance in her life, is always trying to find time to go to the gym, can never keep up with emails, Facebook or Twitter and tries to write page-turning books that her readers will love.

Connect with Cathryn:
Newsletter https://app.mailerlite.com/webforms/landing/c1f8n1
Twitter: https://twitter.com/writercatfox
Facebook: https://www.facebook.com/AuthorCathrynFox?ref=hl
Blog: http://cathrynfox.com/blog/
Goodreads: https://www.goodreads.com/author/show/91799.Cathryn_Fox

Pinterest http://www.pinterest.com/catkalen/